"I don't want to fight with you, *cara*."

"What *do* you want to do, then?" Juliette should never have asked such a loaded question, for she saw the answer in the dark gleam of Joe's chocolate-brown eyes.

Joe closed the distance between them in a number of slowly measured strides but she didn't move away. She couldn't seem to get her legs to work, couldn't get her willpower back on duty, couldn't think of a single reason why she shouldn't just stand there and enjoy the exquisite anticipation of him being close enough for her to touch.

He lifted his hand to her face and skated his index finger down the curve of her cheek from just below her ear to the bottom of her chin. It was the lightest, barely there touch but every cell in her body jolted awake like a dead heart under defibrillator paddles.

She could see the lines and contours of his sculptured mouth, could remember how it felt crushed to her own.

Oh, his mouth was her kryptonite.

"Take a wild guess what I want to do."

Melanie Milburne read her first Harlequin novel at the age of seventeen, in between studying for her final exams. After completing a master's degree in education, she decided to write a novel, and thus her career as a romance author was born. Melanie is an ambassador for the Australian Childhood Foundation and a keen dog lover and trainer. She enjoys long walks in the Tasmanian bush. In 2015 Melanie won the HOLT Medallion, a prestigious award honoring outstanding literary talent.

Books by Melanie Milburne

Harlequin Presents

The Tycoon's Marriage Deal
A Virgin for a Vow
Blackmailed into the Marriage Bed
Tycoon's Forbidden Cinderella

Conveniently Wed!

Bound by a One-Night Vow
Penniless Virgin to Sicilian's Bride
Billionaire's Wife on Paper

One Night With Consequences

A Ring for the Greek's Baby

Secret Heirs of Billionaires

Cinderella's Scandalous Secret

The Scandal Before the Wedding

Claimed for the Billionaire's Convenience
The Venetian One-Night Baby

Visit the Author Profile page
at Harlequin.com for more titles.

Melanie Milburne

THE RETURN OF HER BILLIONAIRE HUSBAND

HARLEQUIN
PRESENTS

ISBN-13: 978-1-335-14839-1

The Return of Her Billionaire Husband

Copyright © 2020 by Melanie Milburne

Harlequin Enterprises ULC
22 Adelaide St. West, 40th Floor
Toronto, Ontario M5H 4E3, Canada
www.Harlequin.com

Printed in U.S.A.

THE RETURN OF HER BILLIONAIRE HUSBAND

To all the parents who have lost a baby at birth. Your journey through grief is unimaginably painful and long lasting. My thoughts are with you. xx

CHAPTER ONE

THERE WAS A weird kind of irony in arriving as maid of honour for your best friend's destination wedding with divorce papers in your hand luggage. But the one thing Juliette was determined *not* to do was spoil Lucy and Damon's wedding day. Well, not just a wedding day but a wedding weekend. On Corfu.

And her estranged husband was the best man.

Juliette sucked in a prickly breath and tried not to think of the last time she'd stood at an altar next to Joe Allegranza. Tried not to think of the blink-and-you'd-miss-it ceremony in the English village church in front of a handful of witnesses with her pregnancy not quite hidden by her mother's vintage wedding dress. The dress that scratched and itched the whole time she was wearing it. She tried not to think of the expression of disappointment on her parents' faces that their only daughter was marrying a virtual stranger after she got pregnant on a one-night stand.

Tried not to think of her baby—the baby girl who didn't even get to take a single breath...

Juliette stepped down out of the shuttle bus and walked into the foyer of the luxury private villa at Barbati Beach. The scarily efficient wedding planner, Celeste Petrakis, had organised for the wedding party to stay at the villa so the rehearsal and other activities planned would run as smoothly and seamlessly as possible. Juliette had thought about asking to stay at another hotel close by, as she didn't fancy running into Joe more than was strictly necessary. Socialising politely with her soon-to-be ex-husband over breakfast, lunch and dinner wasn't exactly in her skill set. But the thought of upsetting the drill sergeant wedding planner's meticulous arrangements was as intimidating as a cadet saying they weren't going to march in line on parade. Juliette had even at one point thought of declining the honour of being Lucy's maid of honour, but that would have made everyone think she wasn't over Joe.

She most definitely was over him—hence the divorce papers.

'Welcome.' The smartly dressed female attendant greeted her with a smile bright enough for an orthodontist's website homepage. 'May I have your name, please?'

'Bancroft…erm… I mean Allegranza.' Juliette wished now she had got around to officially changing back to her maiden name. Why hadn't she? She still didn't understand why she'd taken Joe's name in the first place. Their marriage hadn't come about the normal way. No dating, no courtship, no professions of love. No romantic proposal. Just one night of bed-wrecking sex and then goodbye and thanks for the memories. They hadn't even exchanged phone numbers. By the time she'd worked up the courage to track Joe down and tell him she was pregnant, he had insisted—not proposed, *insisted*—on marrying her soon after. They'd only lived together as man and wife for a total of three months. Three months of marriage and then it was over—just like her pregnancy.

But once Joe signed the papers and the divorce was finalised she would be free of his name. Free to move on with her life, because being stuck in limbo sucked. How would she ever be able to get through the grieving process without drawing a thick black line through her time with Joe?

She. Had. To. Move. On.

The receptionist click-clacked on the computer keyboard. 'Here it is. J Allegranza. And the J is for…?'

'Juliette.' She wondered if it would be pedantic to insist on being addressed by her maiden name while she was here but decided against saying anything. But why hadn't Lucy told the wedding planner she and Joe were separated? Or were Lucy and Damon still hoping she and Joe would somehow miraculously get back together?

Not flipping likely. They shouldn't have been together in the first place.

If her childhood sweetheart, Harvey, hadn't taken it upon himself to dump her instead of proposing to her, like she'd been expecting, none of this would have happened. Rebound sex with a handsome stranger. Who would have thought she had it in her? She wasn't the type of girl to talk to staggeringly gorgeous men in swanky London bars. She wasn't a one-night stand girl. But that night she had turned into someone else. Joe's touch had turned her into someone else.

Note to self. Do not think about Joe's touch. Do. Not. Go. There.

There was not going to be a fairy tale ending to their short-lived relationship. How could there be when the only reason for their marriage was now gone?

Dead. Buried. Lying, sleeping for ever, in a tiny white coffin in a graveyard in England.

'Your suite is ready for you now,' the receptionist said. 'Spiros will bring your luggage in from the shuttle.'

'Thank you.'

The receptionist handed her a swipe key and directed her to the lifts across the hectare of marble floor. 'Your suite is on the third floor. Celeste, the wedding planner, will meet with the bridal party for drinks on the terrace, to go through the rehearsal and wedding timetable, promptly at six this evening.'

'Got it.' Juliette gave a polite movement of her lips, which was about as close to a smile as she got to these days. She took the key, hitched her tote bag over her shoulder and made her way over to the lifts. The divorce papers were poking out of the top of her bag, a reminder of her two-birds-one-stone mission. In seven days, this chapter of her life would finally be over.

And she would never have to think about Joe Allegranza again.

There was only one thing Joe Allegranza hated more than weddings and that was funerals. Oh, and birthdays—his, in particular. But he could hardly turn down being his mate's best man, even if it meant coming face to face with his estranged wife, Juliette.

His wife…

Hard to believe how those two words still had the power to gouge a hole in his chest—a raw gaping hole that nothing could fill. He couldn't think of her without feeling he had failed in every way possible. How had he let his life spin out of control so badly? He, who had written the handbook on control.

Mostly, he could block her from his mind. Mostly. He binged on work like some people did on alcohol or food. He had built his global engineering career on his ability to fix structural failures. To forensically analyse broken bridges and buildings, and yet he was unable to do anything to repair his broken marriage. Fifteen months of separation and he hadn't moved forward with his life. *Couldn't* move on with his life. It was as if an invisible wall had sprung up in front of him, keeping him cordoned off, blocked, imprisoned.

He glanced at the wedding ring still on his finger. He could easily have taken it off and locked it in the safe, along with Juliette's rings that she had left behind.

But he hadn't.

He wasn't entirely sure why. Divorce was something he rigorously avoided thinking about. Reconciliation was equally as daunting. He was stuck in no man's land.

Joe walked into the reception area of the luxury

villa where the wedding party were staying and was greeted by a smiling attendant. 'Welcome. May I have your name, please?'

'Joe Allegranza.' He removed his sunglasses and slipped them into his breast pocket. 'The wedding planner made the booking.'

The reception attendant peered a little closer at the screen, scrolling through the bookings with her computer mouse. 'Ah, yes, I see it now. I missed it because I thought the booking was only for one person.' She flashed him a smile so bright he wished he hadn't taken his sunglasses off. 'Your wife has already checked in. She arrived an hour ago.'

His wife. A weight pressed down on Joe's chest and his next breath was razor-edged. *His failure* could just as easily be substituted for those words. Hadn't the wedding planner got the memo about his and Juliette's separation?

The thought slipped through a crack in his mind like a fissure in bedrock, threatening to destabilise his determination to keep his distance.

A weekend sharing a suite with his estranged wife.

For a second or two he considered pointing out the booking error but he let his mind wander first... He could see Juliette again. In private. In person. He would be able to talk to her face to face instead of having her refuse to answer his calls or delete or block his texts or emails. She hadn't responded to a single missive. Not one. The last time he'd called her to tell her about the fundraising he'd organised for a stillbirth foundation on their behalf, the service provider informed him the number was no longer connected. Meaning Juliette was no longer connected *to him*.

His conscience woke up and prodded him with a jabbing finger.

What the hell are you thinking? Haven't you done enough damage?

It was crazy enough coming here for the wedding, much less spend time with Juliette— especially alone. He had ruined her life, just like he had done to his mother. Was there a curse on him when it came to his relationships? A curse that had been placed on him the day he was born. The same day his mother had died. His birthday: his mother's death day.

If that wasn't a curse, then what the freaking hell was?

Joe cleared his throat. 'There must be some mistake. My…er…wife and I are no longer together. We're…separated.' He hated saying the ugly word. Hated admitting his failure. Hated knowing it was largely his fault his wife had walked out on their marriage.

The receptionist's eyebrows drew together in a frown. 'Oh, no—I mean, that's terrible about your separation. Also, about the booking, because we don't have any other rooms and—'

'It's fine,' Joe said, pulling out his phone. 'I'll book in somewhere else.' He began to scroll through the options on his server. There had to be plenty of hotels available. He would sleep on a park bench or on the beach if he had to. No way was he sharing a room with his estranged wife. Too dangerous. Too tempting. Too everything.

'I don't think you'll find too much available,' the receptionist said. 'There's several weddings on this part of Corfu this weekend and, besides, Celeste really wanted everyone to stay close by to give the wedding a family feel. She'll be gutted to find out she's made a mistake with your booking. She's worked so hard to make her cousin's wedding truly special.'

Joe's memory snagged on something Damon had told him about his young cousin, Celeste. How this wedding planning gig for her older cousin was her first foray into the workforce after a long battle with some type of blood cancer. Leukaemia? Non-Hodgkin's? He couldn't remember which, but he didn't want to be the one to rain on Celeste's first parade.

'Okay, so don't tell Celeste until I make sure I

can't find accommodation. I'll do a ring around and see what I find.'

He fixed problems, right? That was his speciality—fixing things that no one else could fix.

And he would fix this or die trying.

Joe stepped back out into the sunshine and spent close to an hour getting more and more frustrated when there was no vacancy anywhere. Beads of sweat poured down the back of his neck and between his shoulder blades. He even for a moment considered making an offer to *buy* a property rather than face the alternative of sharing a room with his estranged wife. He certainly had enough money to buy whatever he wanted.

Except happiness.

Except peace of mind.

Except life for his baby girl...

His phone was almost out of charge when he finally conceded defeat. There was nothing available close by or within a reasonable radius. Fate or destiny or a seriously manipulative deity had decided Joe was sharing a room with Juliette.

But maybe it was time to do something about his marriage. Keeping his distance hadn't solved anything. Maybe this was a chance to see if there was anything he could say or do to bring a resolution to their situation. Closure.

Joe walked back into Reception and the young receptionist gave him an I-told-you-so smile. 'No luck?' she said.

'Nope.' Luck and Joe were not close friends. Never had been. Enemies, more like.

'Here's your key.' The receptionist handed it over the counter. 'I hope you enjoy your stay.'

'Thank you.' Joe took the key and made his way to the lift. *Enjoy his stay?* Like that was going to happen. He'd been dreading seeing Juliette again, knowing he was largely responsible for her pain, her sorrow, her devastation. But at least this way, in the privacy of 'their' suite, he would be able to speak to her without an audience. He would say what needed to be said, work out the way forward—if there was a way forward—and then they could both move on with their lives.

CHAPTER TWO

JULIETTE HAD A refreshing shower and was dressed in a luxurious bathrobe with her hair in a towel turban. The bespoke bathrobe—apparently all the wedding party had them—had her initials embroidered over her right breast—JA. Which was a pity because the bathrobe was absolutely divine and she hated the thought of tossing it in a charity bin. But maybe, once she got home, she could unpick the embroidery and embroider JB instead.

The wedding planner had certainly pulled all the stops out. There were handmade chocolates with the bride and groom's names on them by the bedside, plus spring water bottles labelled with a photo of the happy couple. It was hard to look at her friend's blissfully happy smile in that photo and not feel insanely jealous.

Why couldn't she have found a man to love her like Damon loved Lucy?

Juliette had thought her ex, Harvey, had loved her. How could she have been so blind for so long? Harvey had said the three little words so often and yet they had meant nothing.

She had meant nothing.

And Joe hadn't loved her either, but at least he hadn't lied to her about it. Their relationship hadn't been a love match but a convenient solution to the problem of her accidental pregnancy. A duty marriage. A loveless arrangement to provide a secure home and future for their child. She had known it from the start and still married him because she couldn't bear to face the disappointment on her parents' faces. The disappointment she had seen throughout her life—every school report, every exam result, every time she failed to gain their approval. Every time she failed to live up to the standards set by her exceptionally talented, high achieving older brothers. And her parents, with their multiple university degrees. Even her very existence had been a mistake. She was a mid-life baby born to older parents who thought their child-rearing days were over. And they *were* over, so they'd outsourced the rearing of Juliette to a variety of nannies.

Juliette placed her hand on the flat plane of her abdomen, her heart squeezing as she thought of the precious life she had nurtured there for seven months. Her baby might have been an accident but no way would she ever think of Emilia as a mistake. Oh, God, she shouldn't say her name, even in her head. It brought her so much pain, so much anguish to think of Emilia's tiny little crinkled face, her tiny wrinkled legs and arms. Little arms that would never reach up to her to hold...

Juliette turned to the task at hand, determined to keep control of her emotions. She was moving on, processing the grief the best way she could. Part of that process was getting through this weekend and handing over the divorce papers to Joe.

She was still deciding which dress to wear to the drinks and rehearsal and had her choices laid out on the bed. The very *big* bed with cloud-soft pillows and gazillion thread-count Egyptian cotton sheets. It was similar to the bed she and Joe had spent that one-night stand in, having off-the-Richter-scale sex.

A night she couldn't erase from her brain or her body.

She swung away from the bed and snatched up her make-up bag from her open suitcase. She needed armour and not just the cosmetic sort. She needed anger armour. Anger was her friend now. Her constant companion. It simmered and smouldered deep in her chest like lava inside a grumbling volcano. Anger was her way of punching through the blanket of despair that had almost smothered her after losing the baby seven months into the pregnancy. A despair so deep and thick it had taken every particle of light out of her life. Happiness was something other people experienced. Not her. Not now. Not ever. A part of her was missing.

Broken. Shattered.

And all the King's horses and all the King's men were not going to be able to put her back together again.

Juliette was on her way to the bathroom off the bedroom to do her make-up when she heard a brisk knock on the door of the suite. Thinking it was a waiter bringing the pot of tea she had ordered a short time ago, she called out, 'Come in. Just leave it on the table, thanks.' And went into the bathroom and closed the door.

She heard the suite door open and the rattle of a tea cup and saucer as presumably the tea trolley was wheeled in. Then the door closed again with a firm click.

Should she have given the waiter a tip? Probably not while she was dressed in a bathrobe, even if it was the most deliciously soft fabric she had ever worn against her skin. Not that she had too much spare cash lying around for tips. She refused on principle to touch the obscenely excessive amount of money Joe put in her bank account every month. Guilt money? No. Those were relief funds. *His* relief. He hadn't got there in time for the birth, but when he came in half an hour later she hadn't seen a father grieving for his stillborn baby girl. She had seen relief washing over his features. She had seen a man who was relieved his sham of a marriage now had an excuse to end.

Their baby had died and so had any hope of them remaining together.

They were a mismatch from the start. Hadn't she always known that on some level? He was suave and sophisticated and super intelligent. A self-made man who answered to no one but himself. His cool aloofness had drawn her like a moth to a dangerously hot flame.

And it had burned her in the end. Even after three months living together as man and wife, he had always kept an emotional distance, which had reinforced every fear she harboured about herself. It mirrored the emotional distance she'd experienced from her parents while she was growing up. The sense she wasn't enough for them—not clever enough, not pretty enough. She always felt they were holding back, keeping her to one side, *compartmentalising* her.

Juliette picked up her foundation bottle, took off the lid and released a sigh. Joe had done the same.

He had travelled abroad for most of the time they were married, leaving her stranded at his villa in Positano. As far as she could see, he hadn't made any adjustments to his life by marrying her. He had expected her to do all the adjusting. She had moved countries, left friends and family behind and lived in a large villa with no one for company other than a rotating agency-recruited team of household staff. None of whom stayed long enough for her to learn their names, much less their language.

Juliette picked up her foundation brush and ran her fingers over the soft bristles. Of course, she was always there waiting for Joe when he returned, and she couldn't fault their physical relationship. It was as exciting and pleasurable as ever but it niggled at her that he seemed to spend more time away than he did at home. What did that say about her? Hadn't her parents done the same? So many trips abroad, lecture tours, sabbaticals, leaving her languishing and lonely in boarding school.

Juliette applied some foundation to cover the dark shadows that seemed to be permanently under her eyes. There was nothing she could do about the shadows in her eyes—they were also permanent. She put on some eye shadow and then a coat of mascara but she left the lip-gloss for after she had her cup of tea. She unwound the towel from around her head and shook her shoulder-length hair loose. Looking at herself in the mirror, there was no sign she had ever carried a baby to seven months' gestation. Her weight was back to normal…well, the new normal, because her appetite was hardly what anyone could call enthusiastic these days. Her hair had grown and thickened up again after a lot of it falling out due to hormones and deep emotional stress.

She looked like the same person…but she was not.

Juliette came out of the bathroom and walked into the lounge area and immediately saw the tea trolley next to the table by the window. She heaved a sigh of relief. A proper pot of tea with a silver tea strainer. No musty little tea bags and lukewarm water for this wedding party guest.

Big tick for you, Celeste.

Juliette could smell the bergamot notes of the high-quality Earl Grey in the air…and something else. Something that struck a chord in her memory and made a faint prickling sensation tiptoe across her scalp.

She swung around from the tea tray to see her estranged husband, Joe Allegranza, seated on the sofa behind her. A gasp rose but died in her blocked throat, her hand coming up to her chest to hold her leaping heart in place.

'What the hell are you doing in my room?' Her voice was a fishwife screech, her pulse a thud-stop-thud-stop hammering in her temples.

Joe rose from the sofa, his expression as unreadable as one of her father's astrophysicist research papers. 'It's apparently our room.' His deep baritone with its rich Italian accent made something in her stomach swoop.

Juliette frowned so hard a year's supply of Botox would have given up in defeat. Two years' supply. '*Our* room? What do you mean "our" room?'

'There's been a mistake with the booking.'

She narrowed her eyes to hairpin slits. 'A mistake?' She knew all about mistakes. Wasn't he her biggest one? She wrapped her arms around her middle, wishing she wasn't naked under the bathrobe. Wishing she had more armour against the tall, unknowable man in front of her. She needed heels the size of stilts to get anywhere near his six-foot-four height. She needed her head read for even noticing how gorgeous he looked, dressed in dark denim and a sky-blue open-necked shirt that highlighted his olive complexion.

She drank in his features, hating herself for being so weak. The determined jaw, the slash of aristocratic cheekbones, the ink-black eyebrows over hooded eyes the colour of centuries-old coal.

The sensual mouth that had wreaked such havoc on her senses from the first time he had smiled at her, let alone kissed her.

But she was not going to think about his kisses. No. No. No.

Nor his earth-shattering, planet-dislodging love-making. No. No. No.

What she had to concentrate on was her anger. *Yes. Yes. Yes.*

'Juliette…' His voice had a note of authority that made her spine stiffen. 'The way I see it, we have two options here. We either go downstairs and make a fuss and thereby draw a lot of attention to ourselves, or we suck it up and leave things as they are.'

Juliette unwound her arms from around her middle and widened her eyes to the size of the saucer under her bone china teacup. 'Are you out of your mind? Why can't we go downstairs and tell Reception they've made a monumental error? But wait—isn't this the wedding planner's mistake? Celeste Petrakis was the one who organised the accommodation. She's being paid a ridiculous amount of money to make sure everything runs smoothly. This—' she pointed her finger between him and herself '—is not what I'd call running smoothly.'

A frown drew his eyebrows closer together and

he looked down at one of his rolled-up sleeves and flicked off an imaginary piece of lint. The gold glint of his wedding ring on his finger stopped her heart for a moment. *He was still wearing his wedding ring?* Why? She had left hers at his villa in Positano, but hardly a day went past when her thumb didn't go in search of them on her finger like a child's tongue checking the vacant space left by a missing tooth.

His gaze came back to hers—dark, deep, mysterious. 'Celeste is Damon's cousin. This is her first job after being sick with blood cancer. It would upset God knows how many relatives of his if we make a big deal about this. Greeks are all about family. Besides, this is Lucy and Damon's wedding and I don't want to draw unnecessary attention to our situation.'

Juliette chewed at her lip, knowing there was a lot of truth in what he said. Wedding party guests were meant to be the supportive team, not the main event. And it made sense not to make a fuss, given Celeste's health issues. She admired the girl for getting back out there, and with such focus and dedication. Juliette hadn't been able to illustrate another children's book since she'd lost the baby. Her publisher and editors, and Lucy who co-wrote the books with her, had been incredibly patient but how long would that continue?

'But what if one of us stayed in another room? Another hotel? There are plenty of hotels further down the—'

'No.' There was an intractable tone in his voice. 'I've already spent the best part of an hour trying to find somewhere and drawn a blank. Lucy and Damon wanted the wedding party staying in one place. And there are no other rooms vacant here. So we will have to share.'

Juliette swung away and began pacing the floor, her arms wrapping around her body again. 'This is ridiculous. I can't believe this is happening. A weekend of sharing a suite with you? It's…it's unthinkable.'

'You've shared much more than a suite with me in the past. Our first night together was spent in a room very much like this one, was it not?' His coolly delivered statement triggered a firestorm in her body, sending waves of heat coursing through her flesh.

She didn't want to think about that night and how her body so wantonly, greedily responded to him. How her senses had reeled under the ministrations of his touch. How many women since their breakup had enjoyed the pressure of his mouth, the smooth, hard thrust of his body, the sensual glide of his hands? A hot spear of jealousy drove through her belly, sending pain so deep into her body she only just managed to suppress a gasp.

Juliette sent him a glare hot enough to blister the paint off the walls. 'How many women have you shared a hotel room with since we separated?'

Something moved across his features like a zephyr across a deep dark body of water. 'None. We are still technically married, *cara*.' His voice had a low and husky quality, his eyes holding hers in a lock that felt faintly disturbing. Disturbing because she found it almost impossible to look away.

She frowned, opening and closing her mouth in an effort to find something to say. *None?* No lovers since her? What did that mean?

She swallowed and finally found her voice. 'You've been celibate the whole time? For *fifteen* months?'

His crooked smile made something kick against her heart like a tiny invisible hoof. 'You find that surprising?'

'Well, yes, because you're…' Her words trailed off and her cheeks grew warm and she shifted her gaze.

'I'm what?'

Juliette rolled her lips together and glanced at him again. 'You're very good at sex and I thought you'd miss it and want to find someone else, many someone elses, after we broke up.'

'Have you found someone else?' A line of tension ran from the hinge of his jaw to his mouth.

Juliette gave a choked-off laugh. Her, sleep with someone else? The thought hadn't even crossed her mind. Which was kind of weird, come to think of it. Why hadn't it? She was supposed to be over him. Wouldn't being over him mean she would be interested in replacing him? But somehow the thought of it sickened her. 'No, of course not.'

Joe's eyes were unwavering on hers. 'But why not? You're very good at sex too. Don't you miss it?' His deep and husky tone was like dark rich treacle poured over gravel.

It wasn't just her cheeks that were hot—her whole body was on fire. Flickering flames of re-awakened lust smouldering in each of her erogenous zones. Erogenous zones that reacted to his presence as if finely tuned to his body's radar. Her body recognised him in a thousand and one ways. Even his voice had the power to melt her bones. Her flesh remembered his touch as if it were imprinted in every pore of her skin. Hunger for his touch was a background beat in her blood but every time his gaze met hers it sent her pulse rate soaring.

And she had a feeling he damn well knew it.

Juliette smoothed her suddenly damp palms down the front of her bathrobe, turning away so her back was to him. 'This is exactly why I don't want to share a room with you this weekend.'

'Because you still want me.' He didn't say it as a question but as a statement written in stone.

Juliette turned and faced him, anger rising in her like a pressure cooker about to explode. Her body trembled, her blood threatening to burst out of her veins. Should she mention the divorce papers burning a hole in her tote bag? The thought crossed her mind but then she dismissed it. She planned to hand them to him once Lucy and Damon left on Sunday morning for their yachting honeymoon. It would spoil the happy couple's celebrations if the hideous D word was mentioned.

But Joe had mentioned the other dangerous D word. Desire.

'You think I can't resist you?' Her voice shook with the effort of containing her temper.

His eyes went to her mouth as if he were recalling how she had shamelessly, brazenly pleasured him in the past. His gaze came back to hers and something deep and low in her belly rolled over. 'I don't want to fight with you, *cara.*'

'What *do* you want to do then?' Juliette should never have asked such a loaded question, for she saw the answer in the dark gleam of his chocolate-brown eyes.

Joe closed the distance between them in a number of slowly measured strides but she didn't move away. She couldn't seem to get her legs to work, couldn't get her willpower back on duty, couldn't think of a single reason why she shouldn't just stand there and enjoy the exquisite anticipation of him being close enough for her to touch.

He lifted his hand to her face and skated his index finger down the curve of her cheek from just below her ear to the bottom of her chin. It was the lightest touch, barely there, but every cell in her body jolted awake like a dead heart under defibrillator paddles. Every drop of blood in her veins put on their running shoes. Every atom of her willpower dissolved like an aspirin in water. She could smell the lime notes of his aftershave cologne. She could see the sexy shadow of his regrowth peppered along his chiselled jaw and she had to curl her hands into fists to stop from touching it. She could see the lines and contours of his sculptured mouth, could remember how it felt crushed to her own.

Oh, dear God, his mouth was her kryptonite.

'Take a wild guess what I want to do.' His voice was rough, his eyes hooded, the air suddenly charged with erotic possibilities.

Juliette could feel her body swaying towards him as if someone was gently but inexorably pushing her from behind. Her hands were no longer balled into fists by her sides but planted on the hard wall of his chest, her lower body pulsing with lust-heated blood.

His hands settled on her hips, the warmth of his broad fingers seeping into her flesh with the potency of a powerful drug. His black-as-night gaze went to her mouth and she couldn't stop from moistening her lips with the darting tip of her tongue.

He drew in a sharp breath as if her action had triggered something in him, something feral, something primal. He brought her even closer, flush against his pelvis, and her traitorously needy body met the hard jut of his.

His mouth came down to within millimetres of hers, his eyes sexily hooded. 'This was never the problem between us, was it, *cara*?' His warm hint of mint breath caressed her lips and her willpower threw its hands up in defeat and walked off the job.

Juliette's heart was beating so fast she thought she was having some sort of medical event. 'Don't do this, Joe…' Her voice didn't come out with anywhere near the stridency she'd intended.

He nudged her nose with his—a gentle bump of flesh meeting flesh that sent a wave of longing through her body. 'What am I doing, hmm?' His lips touched the side of her mouth, not a kiss but so close to it her lips tingled all over. He brushed her cheek with his mouth and the graze of his stubble made something hot and liquid spill deep and low in her core.

Juliette's lips parted, her lashes lowered, her mouth moved closer to his but then a stop sign came up in her head. What was she doing? Practically begging him to kiss her as if she was some love-struck teenager experiencing her first crush? She drew in a sharp breath and stepped back, glaring at him.

'What the hell do you think you're doing?' Nothing like a bit of projection to take the focus off her own weakness.

His cool composure was an added insult to the tumultuous emotions coursing through her body. 'I would only have kissed you if you'd wanted it. And you did, didn't you, *tesoro*?'

Juliette wanted to slap his face. She wanted to claw her fingernails down his cheeks. She wanted to kick him in the shins until his bones shattered. But instead her eyes filled with stinging tears, her chest feeling as if it were being squeezed in a studded vice. 'I h-hate you.' Her voice cracked over a lump clogging her throat. 'Do you have any idea how much?'

'Maybe that's a good thing.' His expression went back to his signature masklike state. Unreadable. Unreachable. Invincible.

Why wasn't she shrugging off his hold? Why wasn't she putting distance between their bodies? Why was she feeling as if this was where she belonged—in the warm protective shelter of his arms? Juliette slowly eased back to look up at his face, her emotions so ambushed she couldn't find her anger. Where was her anger? She *needed* her anger. She couldn't survive without it pounding through her blood. She blinked back the tears, determined not to cry in front of him.

'I don't know how to handle this…situation…' She swallowed and aimed her gaze at his shirt collar. 'I don't want to ruin Lucy and Damon's wedding but sharing this suite with you is…' She bit her lip, unable to put her fears into words. Unwilling to voice them out loud, even to herself.

Joe inched up her chin with his finger, meshing his gaze with hers. 'What if I promise not to kiss you. That will reassure you, *sì*?'

No! I want you to kiss me.

Juliette was shocked at herself. Shocked and shamed by her unruly desires. She stepped out of his hold and wrapped her arms around her body before she was tempted to betray herself any further.

'Okay. That's sounds like a sensible plan. Let's decide on some ground rules.' She was proud of the evenness of her tone. Proud she had got her willpower back into line. 'No kissing. No touching.'

Joe gave a slow nod. 'I'm fine with that.' He walked over to the sofa and sat down, hooking one ankle over his muscular thigh.

He was fine with that?

Everything that was female in Juliette was perversely offended by his easy acceptance of her rules. Surely he could have put up a little bit of resistance? But maybe he had someone else he wanted to kiss and touch and make love to now. Maybe he was tired of being celibate and was ready to move on with his life. It had been fifteen months after all. It was a long time for a man in his sexual prime to be without a lover. A tight pain gripped her in her chest and travelled down to tie tight knots in her stomach. Cruel twisting knots that made it hard for her to breathe. If she didn't pull herself into line, her grey-blue eyes would turn green. She had no right to be jealous. She had left their marriage. She had divorce papers in her bag, for pity's sake.

'Good.' Juliette's tone was so clipped it could have snipped through tin. 'But of course, that leaves the tricky problem of what to say to Lucy and Damon when they realise we're sharing a suite.' She walked over to the bar fridge and took out a bottle of water, unscrewing the cap and pouring it into a glass. She picked up the glass and turned to face him. 'Any brilliant suggestions?'

Joe's expression was still inscrutable but she could sense an inner guardedness. His posture was almost too casual, too relaxed, too calm and collected. 'We could say we're trying for a reconciliation.'

Juliette took a sip of water before she gave in to the temptation to throw it in his face. She put the glass down on the counter with a clunk. 'A reconciliation? For a marriage that shouldn't have come about in the first place?'

A knot of tension appeared beside his mouth, his eyes locked on hers in an unblinking hold. 'I wasn't the one who left our marriage.'

Juliette stalked over to the windows overlooking the white crescent of the sand and the turquoise water of the beach below. She took a shuddering breath. 'No, because you weren't fully in it in the first place.'

The silence was so long it was as if time had come to a standstill.

She heard the rustle of his clothes as he rose from the sofa. Counted his footsteps as he approached her but she didn't turn around. He came to stand beside her, his gaze focused like hers on the beach below.

After a long moment, he turned his head to look

at her, the line of his mouth bitter. 'If you were to be truthful, Juliette, you weren't fully in it either. You were still getting over your ex. That's why we hooked up in the first place, because you couldn't bear to spend the night he got married to one of your so-called friends, on your own.'

Juliette wished she could deny it but every word he said was true. She had been shattered by Harvey's betrayal. They had been dating since their teens. His affair with Clara had been going on for months and Juliette hadn't had a clue. The night she'd thought Harvey was going to propose to her, he'd told her he was leaving her. Harvey Atkinson-Lloyd, her parents' choice of the perfect son-in-law for their only daughter. The daughter who, unlike their high-achieving sons Mark and Jonathon, had failed to do anything much else to win their approval.

Juliette ground down on her molars, torn between anger at Joe for pointing out her stupidity and anger at herself for making a bad situation worse by falling into bed with him that night.

She turned to face him, chin high, eyes blazing. 'So, what's your excuse for hooking up with me that night? Or do you regularly sleep with perfect strangers when you're working in London?'

An emotion flickered across his face like an interruption in a transmission. A pause. A regroup.

A reset. 'It was the anniversary of my mother's death.' His tone was flat, almost toneless, but there was a stray note of sadness under the surface.

Juliette looked at him blankly. 'But I don't understand... I thought you told me your mother had emigrated to Australia. Wasn't that the reason she wasn't able to come to our wedding?'

'She's my stepmother. Both of my parents are dead.'

Had she misheard him back when they were together? She tried to think back to the conversation but couldn't recall it in any detail. She knew his father had died a few years back but he had barely mentioned his mother. She'd got the sense it was a no-go area for him, so she hadn't delved any further.

They hadn't done much talking about each other's family backgrounds, mostly because he was away such a lot. Their brief passionate reunions when he came home between trips were physical catch-ups, not emotional ones. She had wanted more than physical intimacy but hadn't known how to reach him. Every attempt to get closer to him had failed, with him leaving for yet another work commitment. It was as if he sensed her need for emotional connection and found it deeply threatening. But, to be fair, she too had been pretty sketchy with her own issues to do with her background, not wanting him

to know how out of place she felt in her academically brilliant family.

'I'm sorry...' she said, frowning. 'I mustn't have
heard you correctly when you told me that when
we were living together.'

His lips moved in a grimace-like smile that
didn't involve his eyes. 'My father remarried when
I was a child. But when he died ten years ago,
my stepmother and two half-siblings emigrated
to Melbourne, where she has relatives.'

'Do you have much contact with them? Phone?
Email? Birthdays—that sort of thing?'

'I do what is required.'

Juliette was starting to realise she didn't know
very much about the man she had married in
such haste. Why hadn't she tried a little harder
to get him to open up? Her shock pregnancy had
thrown her into a tailspin. And when she'd finally
worked up the courage to call him and tell him,
he had flown straight to her flat in London with
a wedding proposal. A proposal she had felt compelled to accept in order to mitigate some of the
shame she had caused her parents in getting herself 'knocked up' after a one-night stand.

She looked at him again, wondering how she
could have been so physically close to someone
without knowing anything about him. 'How old
were you when your mother died?'

Joe glanced at his watch and muttered a soft curse. 'Isn't there a drinks thing soon?'

'Shoot.' Juliette gave a much milder version of his curse. 'I'm not dressed and I haven't done my hair.'

He picked up a tendril of her mid-brown hair, trailing it gently through his fingers. 'It looks beautiful the way it is.' The pitch of his voice lowered and his eyes were a bottomless black.

Juliette swallowed and tried hard not to look at his mouth. 'Ahem. You're touching me. Remember the rules?'

He released her hair and stepped back from her with a mercurial smile. 'How could I forget?'

CHAPTER THREE

JOE DROVE A hand through his own hair once Juliette had retreated to the bathroom. No touching. No kissing. Sure, he could abide by the rules. But he hadn't realised it would be as difficult as this. It had been hard enough trying to erase the memory of her touch when he was living thousands of kilometres away. But sharing a suite with her this weekend was going to test his resolve in ways he wasn't prepared for.

He hadn't expected the chemistry to still be there. He hadn't expected the hot, tight ache of desire to grip him so brutally. He hadn't expected to feel anything other than guilt about how things had panned out between them. The guilt was still there, spreading cruel tentacles around his intestines like a poisonous strangling vine. Tentacles that crawled up into his chest and wrapped around his heart and squeezed, squeezed, squeezed like a savage fist.

Truth was, he'd been almost relieved when she hadn't answered his texts and emails. It meant he didn't have to face the train wreck he'd caused. The further along her pregnancy went, the longer he'd stayed away on business. Business others under his employ could have easily seen to. But no, he had wanted—*needed*—to throw himself into the distraction of work, because watching Juliette growing with his child had secretly terrified him. What if she died during childbirth? What if, like his mother, she had a complication and no one could save her?

Had he caused the loss of their baby by not being there? Had his absence caused Juliette unnecessary stress? Hindsight was all very well, but he had thought he was doing the right thing at the time. They weren't in a love relationship. They had married for the sake of the baby and Juliette had seemed okay with that arrangement. Providing stability and security had been his focus.

His focus since their separation had been channelling his efforts into fundraising for a stillbirth research foundation. It had been his way of dealing with his own grief. He considered it far more productive than falling into a heap like his father had done. Joe wanted the money raised to help others, to prevent others from experiencing the devastation of losing a child at birth. Research was expensive and counselling services were always seriously underfunded. But that was changing as a result of his efforts. His own regular large donations along with the fundraising programme he had orchestrated would hopefully reduce the number of stillbirths across the globe.

Joe changed into his fresh clothes and unpacked the rest from his small travel bag and hung them in the wardrobe next to hers. He touched the silk sleeve of one of her tops, lifting it to his nose to smell the lingering scent of her signature perfume. For months after she'd left, he couldn't go into the bedroom they had shared. He'd got his housekeeper to move his things into another room. A room without memories and triggers.

He slid the door closed on the wardrobe, wishing he could lock away his desire as easily. He'd wanted to kiss her. No doubt about that. His lips still burned with the need to feel the soft press of hers. Joe knew he was wrong for Juliette. He was relationship poison. He couldn't seem to help destroying those he cared about. But seeing her again made him realise there was unfinished business between them. Was that why he hadn't made more of a fuss about the booking mix-up? Yes, he'd been concerned about upsetting Damon's young cousin, Celeste, but he might have found some way to resolve the situation even if he had to stay on the other side of the island. And, truth be told, he could have refused the invitation to be Damon's best man in the first place and no one would have blamed him.

But he hadn't because on some level, be it conscious or subconscious, he wanted to be here for the weekend on Corfu with Juliette. On neutral ground. Somewhere where there were no triggers and tripwires to the heartbreak of their past. It suited him to be in close proximity to her, to reassure himself he hadn't totally destroyed her as well as their relationship.

A relationship that might have had a better chance if their baby had lived.

A tight ache spread through his chest when he thought of that lifeless little body. His baby girl with her little wizened pixie face, her tiny feet and hands, her permanently closed eyes.

Was there some sort of curse surrounding him and birth? His own birth had brought about his mother's death. His birthday—the day in the year he dreaded more than any other—was the anniversary of his mother's death. The very same day he had met Juliette in that London bar that had changed both their lives for ever.

The bathroom door opened and Juliette came

out with her hair fashioned in a stylish knot on top of her head. 'Bathroom's all yours,' she said, avoiding his gaze.

Joe swept his gaze over her candy-pink calf-length dress with its waist cinched in with a patent leather belt and her matching high heels that show-cased her slender ankles. He had never met anyone who could look so effortlessly elegant. Whether she was wearing track pants and a sweatshirt or designer wear, she always took his breath away. And when she was naked he forgot to breathe at all. 'You look stunning.'

Her creamy cheeks pooled with colour. 'Thank you.' Her gaze flicked away from his and she moved past him to get to the wardrobe. 'I'll just get my evening purse.'

Joe had to clench his hands into fists to stop himself touching her. The suite wasn't large enough to keep a safe distance. It needed to be the size of a small nation for that. The suite was mostly open-plan with a king-sized bed dominat-ing the bedroom area, with no door between that and the lounge area. No more than a metre or two from the bed was a sofa and single armchair and coffee table and there were minibar facilities near the windows to maximise the view over Barbati Beach. The en suite bathroom was luxuriously appointed but was hardly what anyone would call spacious. For a honeymoon, it would be ideal.

But they weren't on a honeymoon.

Juliette opened the wardrobe and took her purse from one of the shelf compartments. He watched as her eyes went to his clothes hanging next to hers. Saw her teeth sink into her bottom lip and a small frown pull at her forehead.

'Is that against the rules?' Joe asked, leaning against the wall near her. 'To have our clothes touching?'

She stiffened and then shut the wardrobe with a little more force than was necessary. Her cheeks were a fiery red, her grey-blue eyes reminding him of a storm-tossed sea. 'We wouldn't need rules if you would stop looking at me like that.'

'How am I looking at you?'

She pursed her lips and put her chin up at a haughty height. 'Like you want to touch me.'

'I do want to touch you but the rules are the rules.' Joe wanted to touch her so badly it was all he could do to keep his hands under control.

She swallowed and her blush deepened. She dropped her evening purse on the bed and adjusted the belt around her dress. 'I should never have slept with you in the first place. It was totally out of character for me to do something like that.'

'I know it was,' Joe said, pushing himself away

from the wall to approach her. 'That's why that night was so memorable.'

She frowned. 'Are you saying...*you* found it special?'

He gave a crooked smile and, before he could stop himself, he stroked a lazy finger down the curve of her cheek. 'I'd never met someone like you before.'

'Because I wasn't madly in love with you like most women are?' Her eyes glittered with sparks of cynicism.

He traced the outline of her lush mouth, knowing he was breaking the rules but unable to resist the temptation. 'You weren't interested in my money or my status. You just wanted to be distracted from a bad day, just like I wanted to be.'

Her tongue swept over her lips and she gave another audible swallow. 'Joe, we're going to be late for the drinks thing.'

Right now, Joe didn't care if they never made it to their friends' wedding. Being with Juliette—breathing in her scent, feeling the softness of her lips under his fingertip—made his blood pound with longing. A slow drag began pulling at his groin—a primal need he had shut down, ignored, blocked out with work, pulsed to vibrant and undeniable life. He slid his hand to the nape of her neck, meshing his gaze with hers. 'Why aren't you telling me to stop touching you?'

She gave a shuddery breath and her gaze dipped to his mouth. 'I—I don't know…' Her voice was whisper-soft.

He brought up her chin with his finger and locked her gaze with his. 'I'll tell you why, *cara*. Because deep down you want to be touched by me. You think a bunch of silly rules is going to damp down the explosive chemistry we still share?' It certainly wasn't damping down his. Not one little bit. He could feel the electric energy passing between them like a hot fizzing current. He could see it reflected in her eyes—the flicker of her eyelashes, the dart of her gaze to his mouth, the quick sweep of her tongue over her lips.

But then her gaze hardened and she placed her hand around his wrist and pulled it away from her face, shooting him a laser-like glare. 'There is no chemistry. I don't feel a thing where you're concerned. Not a damn thing.'

He captured her hand and tugged her close against his body. 'Want to put that to the test? One kiss. Let's see what happens.'

'Don't be ridiculous.' Her expression was scathing but her tone contained a trace of something else. Something that sounded very much like a dare.

Oh, he dared all right.

Joe breathed in the achingly familiar scent of her, brought his mouth as close to hers as he could without actually touching her lips. 'Just one little kiss.'

'You think I won't be able to help myself, like the night we met? But I can and I will.'

'Prove it.'

Her eyes went to his mouth. 'I don't need to prove anything to you.'

'Prove it to yourself then.'

She wavered for a moment, her eyes going to his mouth and back to his eyes. Then her eyes glazed over with chilly determination. 'Okay. I'll show you how immune I am to you.' She rose on tiptoe and planted a brief chaste kiss on his lips. She lowered her heels back to the floor and gave him an arch look. 'See? No fireworks.'

Joe gave a soft chuckle and released her. 'Probably just as well. I don't think anyone, least of all Damon and Lucy, are going to believe we've reconciled.'

A frown pulled at her brow. 'You're not going to…?' She clamped her mouth shut and turned away to reach for her purse on the bed. 'So, what are we going to tell them?' Her back was turned towards him, her hands fiddling with the clasp on her purse but he could see the tension in her slim back and shoulders as if she was bracing herself for his answer.

'We'll tell them the truth.'

She swung back round to face him, her expression wary. 'The truth?'

'That we're mature adults who are in the process of an amicable separation. Sharing a room for a couple of nights will not be a problem for us.'

Her brows rose. 'Amicable? Not a problem? Funny, but I don't see it quite that way.'

'Think about it, Juliette,' Joe said. 'We could go out there and pretend to be back together and then you'd have to allow me to touch you. Otherwise no one is going to buy it. I'd have to hold your hand, slip my arm around your waist, kiss you. You'd have to lie to your best friend. Is that what you want?'

Her small neat chin came up and her grey-blue eyes pulsated with anger. 'I want this weekend to be over. That's what I want.'

'Yeah, well, I want that too.'

Then maybe he could move on with his life.

CHAPTER FOUR

THE WELCOME DRINKS party was on the terrace in front of the infinity pool that overlooked the beach. The area was decorated with lanterns with golden flickering candles inside and honeysuckle and orange blossom scented the evening air. A champagne tower was on a table festooned with ribbons and posies of flowers on each corner. Two waiters dressed in white shirts, black trousers and black bowties were on standby to hand around a delicious-looking array of finger food. A string quartet was playing at one end of the terrace with a backdrop of cascading scarlet bougainvillea. There was a large sandwich board framed by pink and white flowers with a large love heart in the centre with Lucy and Damon's names written in beautiful calligraphy. Juliette had never seen such a romantic setting and tried not to compare it to her own wedding reception.

There certainly hadn't been any sandwich boards with love hearts on them.

Celeste Petrakis, the wedding planner, a slim young woman in her early twenties with short spiky black hair, was carrying a tablet in her hand and came dashing over to Juliette and Joe as soon as they came out to the terrace.

'Oh, my God, I'm so sorry but I think I've messed up your booking,' Celeste said. 'I only put down one J Allegranza on my list. I don't know how I got that wrong. I know Damon told me you guys were separated but I must have forgotten. Blame it on my chemo brain or something. I'm so embarrassed I want to die.' She clamped a hand over her mouth, her big brown eyes going wide as if she was worried she was going to get struck by lightning by a vengeful God. 'Oops. Didn't mean that. I've spent the last two years trying *not* to do that. But, seriously, I'm awfully embarrassed all the same.'

Joe stood close to Juliette but didn't touch her. 'It's fine, Celeste. We have no problem sharing a room.'

Juliette forced her lips into the semblance of a smile. 'Yes, indeed. So please don't worry, Celeste. You've done a brilliant job of organising everything. I've never seen such a lovely setting for a wedding. It looks like it's going to be an amazing weekend for Lucy and Damon.'

Celeste clasped a hand to her heart, her eyes dewy with emotion. 'Does that mean…? Oh, how romantic! I'm so happy for you both. We'll have a special toast for you guys later toni—'

'No.' Joe's tone was as blunt as a sledgehammer on a slice of sponge cake. 'We're not back together.'

Celeste's face fell and she bit down on her lip. 'Oh…sorry, I misunderstood. Do you want me to organise a fold-out bed for you? I mean, you might not want to share—'

'That would be wonderful, if there's one available,' Juliette said, trying to ignore the magnetic heat of Joe's body within touching distance of hers. If she moved even a fraction of a millimetre her arm would brush against him. It was almost impossible to control the urge to do so.

Touch him. Touch him. Touch him.

The chant was trying to keep up with her racing pulse.

'I'll see what I can do,' Celeste said, glancing between Joe and Juliette as if she couldn't quite work them out. 'I can only apologise again for this stuff-up. I would hate for you to be inconvenienced by my mishandling of—'

'Don't stress,' Joe said, moving slightly, his arm

brushing against the bare skin of Juliette's, sending a shivery sensation through her flesh. 'It's not a problem.'

Juliette moved half a step away and gave the wedding planner a rictus smile. 'We don't want to draw attention away from Lucy and Damon. It's their special weekend, not ours.'

'Thank you for being so amazingly good about it.' Celeste gave them a finger wave and dashed away to greet some other guests coming out to the terrace.

Juliette glanced up at Joe. 'I need to speak to Lucy. She'll stress if she thinks I'm not okay about this. It'll ruin her wedding day for her if she's worrying about me—'

'Then pretend to be okay. It's not that hard.'

She glowered at him. 'Easy for you to say, Mr Show No Emotion.'

Joe shrugged and turned to look at the guests coming out to the terrace. 'It doesn't mean I don't have them.' The bottom register of his voice throbbed with something she had never heard in it before.

Juliette frowned and chewed on the inside of her lip. He was always so aloof and distant. He was like a steep and rocky island she continually circled, looking for a place to anchor.

His eyes met hers in a lock that made the backs

of her knees shiver. 'This weekend could be a blessing in disguise. It could be a chance to sort out some of our issues. Not in the presence of other people, but while we're alone.'

While we're alone.

Juliette had to do everything in her power *not* to be alone with him. The only time she wanted to be alone with him was to hand him those hot-off-the-press divorce papers. 'I don't think our issues are the type that can get sorted out over a weekend, Joe. Not even over a lifetime.'

'Maybe, but at least we should try. I have some regret over how I handled our relationship.'

He had regret? She didn't want to hear about his supposed regret. She had regrets in their multitudes. She had known he had only married her out of duty and she had married him anyway. He had been there for her on his terms, not hers. It had been a fly-in, fly-out marriage that was doomed from the start. Being with him now reminded her of how stupid she had been.

She'd foolishly believed their baby would bond them—would help him fall in love with her as well as their child. She had *wanted* him to love her. Wasn't that every girl's dream? If he had loved her then it would have made her feel better about how they had come together in the first place. It would absolve some of her nagging guilt about her own feelings. She had fallen in lust with him. Simple and bald and blatant as that. Lust was what she still felt for him and it had to stop.

She had to stop fuelling the fire that blazed inside her.

Juliette sent him an icy look. 'There isn't anything you could say to me that would make me want to resume our relationship. Nothing. So don't get any funny ideas that this weekend is going to magically fix what wasn't right in the first place.'

A waiter approached with a tray of drinks and Juliette took a glass of champagne. She was acutely conscious of Joe standing beside her, his arm brushing hers as he reached for a drink sending another hot shiver coursing through her body. Nerves and other emotions she didn't want to think about had her halfway through her drink before Joe had even taken a sip.

'Did you hear me say I want us to get back together?' There was a bite in his tone that nipped at her feminine pride. His eyes were espresso coffee dark and glittering with barely suppressed anger. 'That's the last thing I want.'

Juliette took another sip of champagne and then looked down at the remaining bubbles in her glass. 'Good to know.' It was good, wasn't it? He wanted out. She wanted out. Why then was her chest feeling as if something heavy was pressing all the air out of her lungs? She rapid blinked to clear her suddenly blurry vision, her throat so tight it felt as if a champagne cork was stuck halfway down.

Joe released a long slow breath and moved closer again, resting his hand on the top of her shoulder. The anger had gone from his gaze, to be replaced by a brooding frown. 'I apologise for being blunt but what's done is done and can't be undone.'

Juliette summoned her pride back on duty and brushed off his hand as if it was soiling her dress. 'I thought we agreed not to touch?' Her tone was sharp, her glare cutting.

'Please welcome the bride and groom.' Celeste's cheery voice rang out and the string quartet accompanied Lucy and Damon as they came out onto the terrace to cheers and applause from the assembled guests.

The press of the other guests gathering for a better view brought Joe to stand shoulder to shoulder with Juliette to make more room. Juliette painted a smile on her lips while her elbow landed a surreptitious jab in his ribs. He gave a low grunt that sounded far sexier than she had bargained for and a wave of heat rose over her skin. The steel band of his arm came around her and his hand glided down to her hip in a hold that was blatantly possessive. She glanced at his left hand resting on her hip and saw the gold glint of his wedding ring. The ring that claimed her as his. She was conscious of every point of contact as if her body had been finely programmed to recognise his touch.

She could have been blindfolded and still known it was him.

Lucy and Damon approached arm in arm and with wide smiles. An aura of happiness surrounded them and Juliette wished some of it could brush off on her. Why couldn't she have found happy-ever-after love?

'Oh my gosh, I can't believe my eyes,' Lucy said, grabbing Juliette in a bone-crushing hug that almost spilt the rest of her champagne. 'What's going on? Don't tell me you two are—?'

'No.' Joe's strident tone served to underline the word and land another free kick to Juliette's self-esteem. His arm dropped from around her waist and he added, 'There was a mix-up with the ac-commodation and we're trying to make it easy on Celeste, who double booked the room.'

'Oh, well, then…' Lucy's eyes began to twinkle as brightly as the princess diamond ring on her finger. 'I hope it won't be *too* much of a problem for you sharing?' There was a wink-wink-say-no-more quality to her tone.

'No problem at all.' Juliette kept her features under tight control but she couldn't control the creep of warm colour she could feel pooling in her cheeks. Or the lingering hot tingle on her hip where Joe's hand had rested just moments before.

Damon grinned and grasped Joe's hand. 'Who knows what a weekend on Corfu will do, eh? Great to have you both here to share our special day with us.'

'I wouldn't have missed it for the world,' Joe said with an enigmatic smile.

After a moment or two, Lucy and Damon moved on to greet other guests, and Juliette lifted her glass to her lips and drained it. 'No problem sharing a room. Who knew what a consummate liar I could be? Go me.'

Joe's expression was shadowed by a contemplative frown. 'As I said, we could use this weekend to help both of us move forward.'

She raised her brows, sending him a scathing look. 'And how do you propose we do that? Hmm? Kiss and make up? Thanks, but no thanks.'

He took her empty glass off her and placed it on the stone balustrade nearby. 'It would be a start, don't you think?' His darkened gaze dipped to her mouth as if he were recalling every kiss they had ever exchanged.

Juliette's lips tingled and she fought not to lick her lips to draw any more of his attention to them.

She sent him an arch look. 'That's how we got into this mess, if you remember. You kissed me.'

One side of his mouth came up in a sardonic half-smile. 'I seem to recall you made the first move.'

She ground her teeth so hard she was worried they would turn to powder on the spot. Did he have to remind her how forward and brazen she had been that night? So reckless and out of character. She shot him a pointed glare. 'You didn't have to take me up on it.'

'You seriously overestimate my willpower, *cara*.'

Juliette's chin came up. 'You'd better make sure it's in better shape this time around.'

One of his ink-black brows lifted. 'For when you beg me to take you to bed, you mean?'

Her hands clenched into tight balls by her sides in case she was tempted to slap him. 'Not going to happen.' She injected as much confidence in her tone as she could.

His lazy smile made the base of her spine fizz and tingle. He picked up one of her fists and gently prised open her fingers, his thumb stroking the middle of her palm in a way that was unmistakably sexual. His gaze held hers in a mesmerising lock no amount of willpower to resist could ever have matched. 'You shouldn't be ashamed of our chemistry.' The pitch of his voice lowered to a knee-weakening burr.

Juliette pulled her hand out of his, rubbing at it as if he had burned her. 'I'm not ashamed. I'm disgusted. And for God's sake, stop touching me.'

His smile didn't fade but a line of tension appeared next to his mouth and his eyes hardened. 'Careful, *cara*. We're in public, remember? Sheath those pretty claws until we're alone. Then you can rake them down my back to your heart's desire.'

Juliette had to blink away the scorching-hot images his words evoked. Her body was on fire, swamped with memories of his masterful lovemaking. It had taken her almost two years to be able to reach an orgasm with her ex and even then it was hit and miss thereafter. She had practically orgasmed on the spot the moment Joe kissed her the first time. He never took his pleasure before he satisfied her. He knew her body better than she knew it herself. She had explored every inch of his and, by doing so, had found a passionate and adventurous streak in her personality she hadn't known existed. Standing within touching distance now made her body miss him all the more. She could feel a magnetic pull towards him as if an invisible current of energy was calling her back to base.

To distract herself, she took another glass of

champagne off a passing waiter. She figured it was better to keep her hands and mouth otherwise occupied.

'Do you know any of the other wedding party guests?' Joe asked after a long moment.

Juliette crossed her arms and cupped one hand under her elbow, holding her champagne glass in the other hand. 'Only Lucy. And Damon, of course. I haven't met any of the four other bridesmaids before because they're friends Lucy made since moving to Greece. What about you?'

'I'd heard about his cousin Celeste but not met her before today. But I've met two of the bridesmaids once or twice before.' He took a measured sip of his drink, lowering his glass from his mouth to glance at the view over the terrace.

A dagger of jealousy jabbed her in the gut. 'Oh, really?' Juliette made sure her tone was just mildly interested when in fact she wanted to know dates, times, places and whether he had been to bed with either of them. How could any woman resist him? She certainly hadn't been able to.

Joe turned to look at her with an unreadable expression. 'It's kind of ironic how Damon and Lucy met through us, isn't it?'

'Ironic in what way?'

He gave a one-shoulder shrug and looked down at the contents of his glass, twirling it to set the bubbles spinning. 'They seem pretty happy together. Whether or not it lasts is another thing.'

'Do you have to be so cynical? They're in love. Anyone can see that. That's what we were lacking. We married for all the wrong reasons.'

He didn't respond and instead tipped his glass back and drained it. She couldn't take her eyes off the strong tanned column of his throat and the peppery regrowth on his jaw that, in spite of a recent shave, was already vigorously reappearing. How many times had she felt his stubble against her soft skin? On her face, on her belly, between her thighs…

Juliette suppressed a shudder and turned to look at the other guests milling about for the next part of the entertainment the wedding planner had organised. Which bridesmaids had Joe met before? The blonde one? The sleek raven-haired one? The one with the big boobs and legs that went on for ever?

Joe held out his hand for her empty glass. 'Would you like something soft this time? Orange juice? Mineral water?'

Juliette handed the glass to him, being extra careful not to touch his fingers. 'Are you hinting I might drink to excess and make a fool of myself?'

He drew in a breath and pressed his lips into a flat line before releasing it. 'Look, I know the situation this weekend is hard on you. It's the first time we've seen each other face to face since you left.' His hands were thrust in his trouser pockets, his broad shoulders rolled forward. 'I would have preferred meeting with you in London but you didn't respond to any of my attempts to contact you.'

Juliette had ignored his texts and emails for months. She had even blocked his number on her phone. It had been her way of punishing him for not being there when she'd needed him the most. But in a way she had punished herself because she had made herself completely isolated. Her friends and family had tried to support her but, a few months in, they were all suffering compassion fatigue. Even Lucy, with the distraction of her wedding preparations, hadn't been as available to her, especially since Juliette hadn't felt up to illustrating the books they wrote together since the loss of Emilia. She'd desperately needed to be with someone who knew and understood what she was going through—the grief, the pain, the loss. She looked down at the flagstones at her feet rather than meet his gaze. 'I wasn't ready. I found it too…triggering.'

He moved closer to her and lightly touched the back of her hand with one of his fingers. 'That's completely understandable.' His voice was gentle as a caress and her hand tingled as if it had been zapped by a live current.

Juliette brought her gaze up to meet his. 'Do you think about her?'

His eyes flickered as if he was suffering a deep internal pain and only just managing to control it. 'All the time. That's why I've regularly donated to and been fundraising for a stillbirth research foundation for the last few months. I wanted to do something positive to help others in our situation. If you'd happened to read any emails from me, you would have known about it. I donated money on behalf of both of us.'

A stillbirth research foundation? Juliette's heart contracted. *He had been fundraising for a still-birth foundation?*

The anger she wore like armour dropped away like a sloughed skin, leaving her feeling stripped of her defences. Defences she needed to keep her from getting hurt all over again. She hadn't read any of his emails for the last fifteen months. She had marked them as spam and felt immensely satisfied doing it.

Knowing now he was doing something for others was all very well, but what about helping her through the worst time of her life? She had stood by their baby's grave alone. Time and time again, she had grieved in isolation. 'But I don't get it. You tell me you've donated money and, knowing you, it would be a significant amount, but you haven't once visited her grave since the funeral.'

His mouth went into a tight line. 'Graveyards aren't my thing. I prefer to pay my respects in other ways.'

Every week when Juliette visited her baby's grave, she hoped to see flowers or a card or toy left by Joe. But there was nothing. She couldn't understand it and nor could she forgive it, in spite of his generosity to others. He came to London for work regularly—how hard would it have been to drop by the cemetery and hand-deliver flowers or a soft toy? Or didn't he want to be reminded of their baby and their broken marriage?

'Were you keeping away in case you ran into me?' She couldn't tone down the accusing note in her voice.

He looked down at her with an unreadable expression. His features could have been carved in stone. 'How often do you go?'

'Every week.'

'Does it help your grieving process?'

Juliette blew out a frustrated breath. 'Nothing helps with that. But at least I feel I'm not ignoring her.'

'Is that what you think I'm doing?'

She raised her chin to a combative height. 'Aren't you?'

He drew in another sharp breath and turned again to look at the view. His posture was stiff and tight as if invisible steel cables were holding him upright. 'There's no right way to grieve, Juliette. What works for one might not work for someone else.' He spoke through gritted teeth, his hands thrust back in his trouser pockets.

'And is your grieving process working?'

He turned his head to look at her with a grim expression. 'What do you think?'

Juliette shifted her mouth from side to side and looked away. Trouble was, she didn't know what to think. He had never behaved the way she had expected him to behave. He hadn't expressed the words she had wanted to hear or done the things she had hoped he would do. Their relationship had been based on his sense of duty towards her and the baby, so when the baby was lost there was no reason to stay together. He hadn't given her a good enough reason to continue their relationship. He hadn't expressed any feelings for her. But then, neither had she for him. She had been incapable of expressing anything but profound grief, which had in time morphed into anger.

She schooled her features into coolly impersonal lines and turned to face him again. 'I think you're secretly relieved we no longer have a reason to stay together.'

His jaw worked for a moment and his mouth tightened into a flat line. 'Let's leave that discussion until later. We're at our friends' wedding, remember?' And, without another word, he turned and left her with nothing but the company of the ocean-scented breeze.

CHAPTER FIVE

AFTER THE BRIEF wedding rehearsal Joe made idle conversation with some of the other guests but his mind was stuck on Juliette. He kept searching for her in the knot of people, a tight fluttering sensation going through his chest every time he caught sight of her honey-brown head in the crowd.

He had thought often of going to the cemetery where their baby was buried in England but each time he baulked. His father had dragged him to his mother's graveside to pay his respects on each and every birthday until he was a teenager. It had been a form of torture to stand by that headstone knowing he was the reason his mother was beneath it. No amount of wishing and praying and hoping could bring his mother or his baby daughter back. No number of visits, flowers or cards could undo what was done. He had always found his father's way of grieving a destructive process.

Joe had chosen a different outlet—a constructive way of processing his grief by raising money for the research that would hopefully save lives and, no doubt, relationships.

But now, touching Juliette, standing next to her, breathing in the scent of her stirred his blood and upped his pulse and made him wonder if there was a chance something positive could come out of their situation. The chemistry was still there, as hot and electric as ever. The explosive chemistry that had kick-started their relationship was the one thing he could rely on to get it going again. He felt the pull of it like an invisible force drawing him to her. He'd had to stuff his hands in his pockets to stop reaching for her. He couldn't be in the same room as her without wanting her. Damn it—he couldn't be in the same country without aching with the need to take her in his arms.

Juliette turned and looked at him across the now moonlit terrace and a small creature scuttled through the ventricles of his heart. Girl-next-door-pretty rather than classically beautiful, she still had the power to snatch his breath. Her grey-blue eyes reminded him of a deep stormy sea with shifting shadows. Her slim frame was ballerina-like with a natural elegance of movement. And her skin was pale but she had a dusting of freckles over the bridge of her upturned nose that reminded him of sprinkled nutmeg. Her mouth was a Cupid's bow of pink lushness that drew his gaze like a magnet and he realised with a sharp pang how much he missed her sunshine-bright smile. Not those fake ones she flashed when required but a genuine one that lit up her face and eyes.

Juliette's gaze shifted back to the older couple next to her who were the bride's parents, but Joe could see she wasn't really engaged in the conversation. She kept chewing at her lower lip and fiddling with the clasp of her evening purse as if she couldn't wait for the evening to be over.

And soon it would be over and they would be alone in their suite.

The string quartet was playing dance numbers and several couples were dancing further along the terrace. He remembered the first time he'd danced with Juliette, how she had moved with him with such natural rhythm as if they had been dancing together for years.

Making love had been the same.

After their one-night stand and they had gone their separate ways, he hadn't been able to get her out of his mind. He'd had commitments back in Italy and then another project in Germany but he hadn't stopped thinking about her. And then, out of the blue, she'd called him and told him she was carrying his child. The news had stunned him.

They had used protection but fate had decided to step in and create a new life. A life that hadn't lasted long enough to take a single independent breath.

Joe let out a long sigh as the familiar pain seized his chest whenever he thought of his tiny baby daughter. He blamed himself for not being there when Juliette went into early labour. Perhaps if he had been there to take her to hospital earlier things might have panned out differently. There were so many things he wished he had done differently.

Joe wove through the small crowd to join her, taking one of her hands in his. 'Would you like to dance?' He figured it was one way he could legitimately hold her in his arms. And, more importantly, stop her from dancing with anyone else.

She looked as if she were about to refuse, but then she shrugged, not quite meeting his gaze. 'Sure. Why not?'

Joe led her to the part of the terrace set up for dancing, overlooking the ocean below. The string quartet was now playing a romantic ballad and he gathered her close, moving with her to the slow rhythm of the music. 'You didn't look like you were enjoying the conversation you were having back there,' he said, breathing in the flowery scent of her hair.

Juliette glanced up at him with a frown. 'Was it so obvious?'

'Only to me.' He led her further away from the other guests who had joined them on the dance floor. 'Do you know Lucy's parents well?'

'Pretty well. I spent a fair bit of time at their house when Lucy and I were teenagers.' She gave a little sigh and added, 'I was really envious of her. Her parents were so different from mine.'

'In what way?'

She didn't respond for so long, he wondered if she hadn't heard him. But then she aimed her gaze at his shirt front and spoke in a low tone. 'They were so…so uncritical. I don't think I've ever heard them say anything negative about her or the choices she made.'

Joe eased back to look down at her. 'And your parents were critical and negative?'

She gave a little eye-roll and lowered her gaze back to his shirt front. 'Not so much when there's an audience. They're way too polite and subtle for that. But I know how much I've disappointed them by not being as academically gifted as them and my two older brothers.'

Joe couldn't say he was all that surprised by her confession. But it niggled him that he hadn't drawn her out a little more on her family while they were living together. What did that say about him? What sort of husband didn't show an interest in his wife's background?

A husband with a troubled background of his own who wanted no questions asked, that was who.

Joe had only met her parents and brothers twice—at the wedding and then Emilia's funeral. The funeral was a bit of a blur to him and they hadn't been particularly warm towards him at the wedding—but he hadn't been expecting them to welcome him with open arms. They'd been polite in a stiff upper lip kind of way, but then his courtship of their only daughter hadn't exactly been ideal. A one-night stand pregnancy was hardly the way to impress and win over in-laws but he hadn't wanted his child to grow up without knowing him. Marriage had been the best option in his opinion.

Their child had to come first—the baby had been his top priority.

Her parents hadn't come to the hospital when they'd lost the baby as they were on a long-haul international flight. Juliette had flown to England to visit her parents before they'd left for a three-month tour abroad. She had been booked on a flight back to Italy the next day when she'd gone into labour. He'd flown back as soon as he heard but he got there too late.

'But you're so talented, Juliette. Your illustrations are amazing. Aren't they proud of your work?'

Her gaze was downcast, her mouth downturned. 'I'm the only person in my family without a PhD. I barely scraped through my GCSEs. A children's book illustrator isn't what they consider a worthwhile career, especially as I don't even have an art degree. They're proud I've had stuff published, sure, but they still see it as a kind of hobby.' She gave another sigh that made her slim shoulders go down. 'I haven't done a sketch in months so maybe they're right. It's time to find something else. I don't know how Lucy has put up with me this long. It's not just my career on hold, but hers too.'

Joe placed one of his hands along the curve of her creamy cheek, meshing his gaze with her troubled one. 'You don't need to think about a career until you're ready, *cara*. I've been depositing funds in your bank account to more than cover any loss of income.'

A tinge of pink spread across her cheeks but a determined light came into her eyes. 'I don't want or need your money. I haven't touched a penny of it.'

Joe brushed his thumb pad across the small round circle of her chin. 'You hate me that much?'

Something flickered in her gaze until her lashes came down over her eyes to lock him out. 'I never wanted your money. That wasn't why I married you.' She stepped out of his hold and crossed her arms over her body as if she were cold but the night air was balmy and warm.

'Yes, well, we both know why you married me.' Joe couldn't remove the cynicism from his tone in time. 'You wanted to show your cheating ex you'd moved on.'

She pressed her lips into a flat line, the colour in her cheeks darkening. 'That's not true. It had nothing to do with him. I can barely remember what he looks like now. I thought I was doing the best thing by the baby by marrying you. Anyway, you were the one who insisted on marriage. I would've been just as happy with a co-parenting arrangement.'

'Have you heard from your ex? Do you ever see him?' Joe wasn't sure why he was asking because he didn't want to know. He could do without the punishment, the torture, the despair of imagining her with someone else. He had never considered himself the jealous type. But the thought of her being intimate with someone else made his gut churn. The thought of her having another child with someone else sent a tight band of pain across his chest until he could hardly draw a breath.

Juliette flashed him an irritated look. 'I hardly see how it's any of your business who I see or don't see.'

Joe led her by the elbow away from the other dancers to a quieter part further along the terrace. 'It's my business because we're still legally married.'

He lowered his hand from her elbow but he had to summon up every bit of willpower he possessed to stop from pulling her back into his arms and crashing his mouth down on hers. To remind her of the passion that sparked between them. The passion that was charging the atmosphere even now.

Which brought him to a perplexing question— what the hell was he going to do about it? He had already made mistakes with Juliette. Big mistakes. Mistakes that couldn't be undone. Would it be asking for trouble to revisit their relationship? To see if it was worth salvaging?

Her gaze glittered with defiance. 'I find it highly amusing how you're suddenly so interested in my private life after all these months.' She glanced at his mouth as if she was expecting him to do what he was tempted to do. 'And why do you keep wearing your wedding ring? It seems rather pointless.'

Joe reached for her left hand, running his thumb over her empty ring finger. He was expecting her to pull away but, surprisingly, she didn't. Instead her gaze meshed with his and her tongue darted out to sweep across her lower lip, her throat rising and falling over a swallow.

'It's not entirely pointless. It keeps me free of unwanted female attention.' He waited a beat before continuing. 'I still have your wedding and engagement rings.' Joe wasn't sure why he was telling her that snippet of useless information. Did it make him sound like a sentimental fool who hadn't got over the walk-out of his wife? Should he tell her he hadn't removed one article of her clothing from his wardrobe? That he couldn't even use the same bedroom they had shared as it caused him too much gut-wrenching pain? And don't get him started on the nursery. He hadn't opened that door once. Not once. Opening that door would be tearing open a deep and devastating wound.

Juliette glanced down at their joined hands before returning her gaze to his. 'I'm surprised you haven't pawned them by now or found someone else to give them to.'

Joe stroked the soft flesh of her palm, watching as her pupils flared and her breath quickened. 'They belong to you.'

Her chin came up, an intransigent light sparking in her eyes. 'I don't want them.'

'Maybe, but still you want me.' Joe brought her hip to hip to his body, his gaze lowering to her mouth. 'Don't you, *mio piccolo*?'

Juliette licked her lips again, her eyes flicking to his mouth. 'No.' Her tone was firm but her body swayed towards him as if propelled by a force bigger than her will to resist.

He tipped up her chin, stroking her lower lip with his thumb. 'Pride is a funny thing, is it not? I would like to say I don't want you either but I would be lying to myself as well as you.'

She drew in a breath and released it in a shuddery rush. 'Joe...please...'

'Please, what?' Joe cupped one side of her face with his hand, the other hand going to the small of her back to bring her even closer to the throb and ache of his lower body. 'Are you going to deny what you're feeling right now? What you've felt from the moment I walked into the suite this afternoon? What you felt the first time we met? It's why you blocked my phone and emails, isn't it? You don't want to be reminded of what you feel for me.'

Juliette swallowed again, her hands creeping up to rest against his chest, her gaze homing in on his mouth. 'We're separated now and—'

'We're not separated this weekend. We're sharing a room. Sharing a bed.'

'No, we're not.' Her hands fell away from his chest, her gaze defiant. 'Celeste said she was going to get a fold-out for—'

'I spoke to her a few minutes ago,' Joe said. 'She wasn't able to get one in time for tonight but she'll try again tomorrow.'

Her gaze flicked back to his, the line of her mouth pulling tight. She stepped back, her posture stiff, guarded. 'We both need to move on with our lives. It would only complicate things to go backwards instead of forwards.'

She placed her left hand against her temple and closed her eyes as if in silent prayer. 'Please, Joe. Don't make this harder than it needs to be.' She lowered her hand from her face and looked up at him again with an expression that shone anew with determination. 'I'm going back to the room. To sleep. *Alone.*'

Juliette managed to slip away without any of the wedding party noticing and went back to the suite and closed the door with a heavy sigh. She'd been so tempted to dance with Joe all night, to find any excuse to be in his arms again. But that was the pathway to heartbreak because they didn't belong together. Not then. Not now.

If only her body didn't keep betraying her. It was so hard to keep her distance when he only had to look at her and her resistance melted. She had lowered her guard enough to tell him about her frustrating relationship with her parents and her doubts over her career going forward. It was a moment of weakness and yet she had drawn comfort from sharing so openly with him. He had been supportive and understanding in a way she hadn't expected.

And then there was the stillbirth foundation…

She couldn't get it out of her mind—how he had raised money for much-needed research. That all this time she had been judging him for not grieving the way she expected, but he'd been doing what he thought would help others. It made it harder for her to access her anger, to keep her emotional distance.

But it didn't mean they had a future together.

How could they when they weren't in love, had never been in love and would only be together for the sake of physical chemistry? That wasn't enough to build a marriage on, especially a marriage that had suffered such a tragedy as theirs. A marriage that would never have come about if it hadn't been for her accidental pregnancy. She wasn't the type of woman he normally dated. She wasn't sophisticated or super-smart and no one could ever call her supermodel beautiful. She would never have been his first choice of bride if she hadn't fallen pregnant.

Juliette pulled the clips out of her hair and tossed them on the dressing table on her way to the bathroom. Joe's shaving things were on the bathroom counter and his bottle of cologne right next to her cosmetics. A soft fluttering sensation passed over the floor of her belly. Sharing a bathroom was such an intimate thing to do. Would she be strong enough to resist the temptation he offered? She picked the cologne bottle up, took off the lid and held the neck of the bottle to her nose, closing her eyes to breathe in the citrus notes. She put the bottle back down and put the lid back on.

She had to be strong enough.

She *had* to.

Juliette came back out to the bedroom and glanced at her tote bag, where the divorce papers were stashed. On Sunday, after Lucy and Damon sailed off, she would whip them out and wave them under Joe's nose, not before. It gave her a sense of power to know she had them there, waiting for the right moment. He thought he could snap his fingers and she would come running back to him as if nothing had changed. Everything had changed.

She had changed.

And she wasn't changing back.

Joe came back to the suite later that night to find Juliette asleep in the bedroom with a bank of pillows dividing the king-sized bed in two sections. The bedside lamp was still on and the muted light cast her features into a golden glow. She had taken her hair down and it was spread out over the pillow. Her make-up was removed, leaving her skin as fresh and glowing as a child's. Her mouth was relaxed in sleep, her lips softly parted, her breathing slow and even. He reached up and loosened his tie, slipping it from around his collar and tossing it to the chair in the corner of the bedroom.

Juliette's eyes sprang open and she sat upright, blinking at him owlishly. 'Oh, it's you...'

'Thanks for the hearty welcome.' Joe began to unbutton his shirt.

Her gaze narrowed and she pulled the bedcovers further up her body. 'What are you doing?'

'What do you think I'm doing?' He shrugged off his shirt and tossed it in the same direction as his tie. 'I'm getting undressed.'

'Can you do it in the bathroom?' Her cheeks were a bright shade of pink and her eyes kept avoiding his. 'And please wear boxers or something. And stay on that side of the bed.'

'It's a bit late to be shy, *tesoro*. I'm familiar with every inch of your body, as indeed you are with mine.'

She threw back the covers and dived for the bathrobe that was hanging over the back of another chair. He caught a tantalising glimpse of café-latte-coloured satin shortie pyjamas, one of the shoestring straps on the camisole top slipping off her shoulder to reveal the upper curve of her breast. She thrust her arms in the bathrobe's sleeves and knotted the waist ties around her middle with unnecessary force, sending him a scalding glare. 'Fine. Have it your way. You have the bed and I'll sleep on the sofa.' She began to stalk past him but he caught her wrist on the way and stalled her passage.

'Don't be so dramatic.' He let her arm go, opening and closing his fingers to ease the tingling sensation touching her had produced. 'I'm not going to force myself on you. You have the bed. I'll take the sofa.'

She bit down on her lip and glanced towards the other section of the suite where the smallish sofa was situated. 'You're too tall for it. You won't sleep a wink.'

He wasn't going to sleep a wink anyway, not with her so temptingly close. Seeing her all sleep tousled with so much of her creamy skin on show was already stretching the limit of his self-control. 'I'm sure we can manage to share a bed for two nights without crossing any boundaries.'

She fiddled with the waist ties of her bathrobe, her teeth still worrying her lip. 'Okay. But you have to promise not to touch me.'

He placed his hand on his heart. 'You have my solemn word.'

Juliette pursed her lips, her gaze searching his for a moment. 'Why do I get the feeling you're laughing at me?'

He lowered his hand from his chest and dropped it back down by his side. 'Believe me, *cara*. It's been a long time since I laughed.'

Her eyes fell away from his and a shadow crossed her features. She turned back to the bed and climbed back under the covers, pulling them up to her chin and turning her back to him. 'Goodnight.'

Joe's gaze went to the box of sleep medication on her bedside table. He came over to her side of the bed and perched on the edge. 'How long have you been taking those?' He pointed to the medication sitting next to a glass of water.

Juliette turned over onto her back, her expression defensive. 'I only use them when I can't sleep.'

'And how often is that?'

Her eyes shifted out of reach of his and her fingers began plucking at the hem of the sheet. 'More often than not...' Her voice was hardly more than a whisper.

Joe stroked back a strand of hair from her forehead, his chest so tight he could barely inflate his lungs to breathe. Guilt rained down on him over how he had handled the last few months. She had suffered alone when he should have been by her side. He'd thought keeping his distance was what she wanted but it clearly hadn't helped her through the grieving process. It certainly hadn't helped him either. So many platitudes sprang to his lips—like the irritating comments other people had made to him.

Time is a great healer.

It will get easier.

You'll be stronger for it.

Instead, he stayed silent.

Her shimmering gaze met his and his chest tightened another painful notch. 'I can't help blaming myself. Maybe I shouldn't have flown home to England to visit my parents before they went on their trip. I didn't need to go. I could have asked them to visit me instead.'

And why had she flown home to England? Because he'd been away on yet another work commitment, leaving her to fend for herself. If anyone was to blame, it was him. Joe took one of her hands and anchored it to his aching chest. 'No. You mustn't blame yourself.' His voice was so rough it could have filed through metal. 'You had a dream pregnancy up until then.'

Her mouth twisted. 'You weren't there for the first three months. It wasn't such a dream pregnancy then. I was sick just about every day.'

Joe wished he had been there but she hadn't

told him until she was twelve weeks along. He laid her hand on his thigh, moving his thumb over the back of her hand in slow soothing strokes. 'I was going to contact you so many times after we slept together that night.'

A frown creased her smooth brow. 'Were you? You never told me that before.'

Joe gave a wry half-smile. 'We hadn't exchanged numbers but I managed to find your details online because of your publishing career. I thought of emailing you numerous times, suggesting we meet up for a drink or something.'

'Why didn't you?'

'You were still getting over your ex. I didn't think you were ready to move on.'

She lowered her gaze and slipped her hand out of his hold and grasped the edge of the bedcovers. 'I think I was over Harvey as soon as he told me he was in love with Clara. But you would've only been offering a fling back then, not something lasting.' She issued it as a statement rather than a question.

Joe stood from the bed and looked down at her, unwilling to confirm or deny it. He had never felt the need to settle down with anyone long-term. He'd preferred to live in a world outside permanent attachment. A safe world. A world where he couldn't hurt or be hurt in return. 'Try and get some sleep, *cara*. Goodnight.'

Juliette listened while Joe had a shower in the bathroom. She tried to stop her mind filling with images of him under the hot spray of water, tried to stop thinking of the times she had shared a shower with him in the past. The blistering passion, the drumming need, the explosive orgasms.

She groaned under her breath and turned so her back was facing the bathroom, tucking her legs up close to her torso and squeezing her eyes shut. She waited for him to join her in the bed, waited for the familiar press of his weight down on the mattress, her senses so alert she knew it would be impossible to settle into sleep. She opened her eyes and saw the medication next to her glass of water. She sat up, pressed one out of the blister packet and swallowed it down with a gulp of water.

She lay back down and waited for the slow but inexorable drag down into mindless slumber...

CHAPTER SIX

JULIETTE DIDN'T KNOW how long she had been asleep when she woke. It was still dark except for a beam of silvery moonlight peeping through a gap in the curtains, illuminating the bed...*the half empty bed.* She sat up and pushed her hair away from her face and frowned at the vacant space beside her. The pillows were undented, the sheets smooth, showing no sign Joe had even momentarily lain down beside her.

A perverse sense of pique washed over her. Why hadn't he slept beside her? Did he find her repulsive? Was he worried she might cross to his side of the bed? She pushed off the bedcovers and, ignoring the bathrobe laid over the chair, padded through to the sitting room area.

Joe was sitting in a slumped position on the sofa, his long legs stretched out in front of him, his head on one side, his eyes closed in a deep sleep.

He was naked except for a bath towel anchored around his lean hips.

Juliette knew she should tiptoe back to bed. Knew she shouldn't feel a smidgeon of compassion for him for having spent an uncomfortable night sleeping upright. Knew she had no right to stare at his tanned athletic body bathed in moonlight, making him look like a Greek god rather than human. But her feet seemed to be anchored to the floor, her eyes drawn to him with the force of an industrial-sized magnet.

She wasn't aware of making a sound but suddenly his eyes opened and he blinked and sat upright, scraping a hand through his already tousled hair.

'Was I snoring?' he asked with a grimace.

'No. Is that a new habit you've acquired since we…?' She left the sentence hanging but couldn't explain why. He'd told her there'd been no one else since she'd left but one day there would be. That was something she didn't want to think about too closely. Someone else in his life. In his bed. In his arms. Experiencing the mind-blowing passion she missed to this day.

Joe drew his legs to a right-angled position, leaned forward and rested his forearms on his thighs. 'Not that I know of.'

There was a moment of silence. A silence so

loaded the air seemed to be weighted, making it hard for Juliette to breathe.

'Why didn't you sleep in the bed?'

Joe lifted his head to look at her, his eyes so dark they could have been black holes in space. 'I didn't want to disturb you. You looked like you needed your sleep.' His voice had a rough edge that made something in her belly lose its footing.

Juliette rolled her lips together and came a little closer, drawn to him as if her body had a will of its own. 'Joe…it's okay if you want to share the bed. Really, we're both mature adults and—'

'It's fine. I got a couple of hours. It's all I need.' He rose from the sofa, securing the towel around his hips, and walked over to the windows, pushing the curtains further aside to look at the moonlit view.

She couldn't take her eyes off the sculpted perfection of his back and shoulder muscles, taut buttocks and his long strong thighs and calves below the hip-height towel. Just knowing he was naked under that towel was enough to send her female hormones into a cheerleading routine. Sensations stirred low in her body—sensual, erotic memories of his thick, hard presence moving within her.

Joe turned from the window and brushed his hair back from his forehead. 'Go back to bed, Juliette.' His tone was part stern authority and part growing impatience.

Juliette took a step towards him. 'Joe...'

He closed the distance between them and placed his hands on the tops of her shoulders. The warmth of his fingers seeped into her flesh, awakening needs and desires she wasn't sure she could control. His hooded eyes drifted to her mouth, his breath hitching, his body so close her breasts brushed against his chest. The smooth satin of her shortie pyjamas couldn't hide her body's reaction to him. She could feel the tensing of her nipples, the spreading tingles in her breasts, the smouldering heat in her core.

His hand cupped one side of her face, his thumb moving across her cheek like the arm of a slow-beating metronome. 'Kissing you would be the easy part. Stopping at one kiss, however, would be something else.' His voice was so rough it sounded as if he'd been gargling with gravel.

Juliette's gaze lowered to his sensually shaped lips and something in her stomach fell off a high shelf. 'Who said I wanted you to kiss me?' Her voice was too breathy to relay the cool indifference she'd aimed for.

One side of his mouth tipped up in a crooked smile that did serious damage to her resolve to resist him. His thumb stroked across her lower lip, back and forth in a mesmerising, spine-tingling rhythm. 'When I arrived here this weekend I was so determined I wasn't going to do this.'

Juliette hadn't realised she'd moved until she found herself flush against him, the hard jut of his hips, the proud rise of his male flesh setting her body on fire. 'Do what?' Her voice was so soft it could barely be called a whisper.

'You know exactly what.' And his mouth came down and covered hers.

Juliette knew she should have pulled away right then. She should have stopped it from going any further. She shouldn't have allowed herself to be tempted, much less give into it. But as soon as his lips met hers, something hard and tight and bitter inside her collapsed like a house of cards. His lips moved against hers in an exploratory fashion, as if he was reminding himself of her contours, her taste, her texture. She groaned and opened to him and his tongue met hers in an erotic dance that made the hairs on the back of her neck tingle and the base of her spine fizz.

Her hands moved from his chest to link around his neck, her fingers playing with the thick black strands of his hair. He made a low growling sound deep in his throat and changed position, deepening the kiss until the bones in her legs threatened to melt like candlewax in a cauldron.

Joe's hands framed her face, his breathing almost as hectic as hers. After long breathless moments he lifted his mouth off hers, gazing down at her for an infinitesimal pause before sealing her lips once more with a softly muttered curse, as if he too hated himself for his weakness where she was concerned.

One of his hands left her face and went to the small of her back, pressing her closer to the tantalising ridge of his male flesh. His other hand went to the nape of her neck, his long fingers splayed into the tingling roots of her hair. Shivers coursed up and down her back, her inner core hosting a welcome party, darts of pleasure shooting between her legs.

Joe lifted his mouth off hers and placed his hands on her hips, stepping back from her a fraction. 'I think it might be time to stop.' Something in his tone belied his words—the gruffness, the rueful note, the chord of longing so low she might have missed it if she hadn't been feeling it herself.

Stop? Now?

When her body was screaming for the release it craved? And why the hell hadn't *she* been the one to stop this madness? She felt hot shame flushing into her face and she shoved his hands off her hips and stepped further back, chest heaving as if she were an affronted heroine in a period drama.

'What the hell do you think you're playing at, kissing me like that?'

One of his ink-black eyebrows rose in a sardonic arc. 'I could ask you the same question.'

Juliette couldn't hold his gaze and swung away. 'I'm going to have a shower. It'll soon be time to get up and get ready for the wedding anyway.' She strode into the bathroom and locked the door, leaning back against it with a ragged sigh. Why had she allowed him to prove how weak she was? How vulnerable to his touch? How lacking in immunity?

How dangerously ambiguous her feelings…

The wedding was to be held in the morning on the beach. Somehow Juliette had managed to shower and dress without running into Joe. He had left the suite while she was in the shower, and because she was heading to Lucy's room for a hair and make-up session with the other bridesmaids she didn't expect to see him again until the ceremony.

Lucy handed Juliette a glass of champagne on arrival. 'Get that into you. Now, tell me how last night went. Did you guys kiss and make up?'

Juliette took the champagne but decided against taking anything but a token sip. 'Let's talk about you, not me. Are you nervous?'

Lucy beamed. 'Me? Nervous? I can't wait to marry Damon.' Her smile dimmed a little. 'I just wish things were better between you and Joe. Are you sure there's no hope of a reconciliation?'

'It's not what either of us wants.'

'Are you sure about that? I saw the way he was watching you last night. He could barely take his eyes off you. And when you two were dancing, well, anyone would have thought you were—'

'We're not.' Juliette's tone was emphatic. She opened the long narrow box that contained Lucy's hand-embroidered veil. 'He slept on the sofa.'

'Oh…'

Juliette turned to look at her friend. 'I don't want your wedding to be spoilt by my dramas with Joe.' She painted a bright smile on her face. 'Now, let's get you ready to marry the man of your dreams. Your dress looks amazing, by the way.'

Lucy twirled this way and that in her voluminous tulle and satin dress. It made her mixed-race complexion look all the more stunning. 'You don't think I look too much like a meringue?' There was a dancing light in her eyes. 'It was a toss-up between this one and the figure-hugging one we looked at together in Mayfair but I've always wanted to be a princess for a day.'

'You look exactly like a princess,' Juliette said, trying to ignore a tiny jab of envy. 'A princess in love.'

* * *

Joe stood next to Damon under the canopy of tropical flowers that had been set up on the beach. He was trying not to think of his own wedding, how different it was from this one. If he and Juliette had married in a more relaxed and informal setting, would it have helped? His goal had been to get married to her as soon as possible for the sake of the baby. The cold and austere village church where generations of her family had been christened, wed or buried would not have been his first choice. But he had wanted Juliette to feel supported by her family, given he had none to speak of.

Damon nudged him. 'Here they come.'

Joe turned and saw Juliette leading the way up the flower-strewn red carpet that had been laid down on the sand. She was dressed in a deep blue satin dress the colour of the ocean that pulsed nearby. The dress clung to her body like a slinky glove, outlining the gentle swell of her hips, the narrow waist, the slight globes of her breasts. There was a garland of flowers in her hair, giving her an *A Midsummer Night's Dream*, almost ethereal look. His chest tightened, his breath stalled, his guilt throbbed. He had failed her in so many ways. He had made promises to love and protect her but he had failed on both counts. Romantic love was something he had never committed to. He doubted it even existed except perhaps in rare cases.

It had certainly never existed for him.

But seeing Juliette walking towards him now, something shifted in his chest. A slippage. A softening. A tightly locked space slowly opening...

He snapped it shut. *Bang.* Bolted the door.

He was comforted by the all too familiar jolt of his emotions shutting down. It was safer not to feel too deeply. To leave stray feelings unexplored. To deny them access through the firewall of his control tower.

Juliette met his gaze and a tremulous smile formed on her lips. The soft lips he had kissed early that morning and only just managed to stop kissing before he lost control. Kissing her made him realise how dangerous it was to be around her. It made him want her. Need her. Crave her. But how could he hope for a rerun of their relationship? What right did he have to insist on a second chance? It would only cause more pain, more heartache. It was practically his brand—projecting pain, heartache and loss onto the people he cared about. It was better he didn't care. It was better he didn't want. It was better not to hope.

Her gaze moved away and a sense of disappointment sank in his stomach like a stone.

Her smile was for the crowd, for appearances' sake.

It wasn't for him.

Juliette couldn't look at Joe without blushing over their kiss that morning. She couldn't look at him and not think about their own wedding. Their cold and duty-bound wedding where the promises he made had meant nothing.

But had hers meant something? Anything? Juliette gave an inward frown, wondering why her conscience was bringing this up now. She hadn't been the one to insist on marriage. She had done the right thing in telling him he was to be a father, to give him the option of being involved or not. She could have refused his offer… *Why hadn't she?*

Juliette stood to one side of Lucy and Damon as they exchanged their vows. Both had tears shining in their eyes, their love for each other plain to see. She glanced at Joe to find his gaze trained on her, his expression grave. She bit her lip and looked away again, her heart feeling as if squeezed by an invisible hand.

Maybe she had judged Joe too quickly. Hadn't her parents always complained about her impulsive nature? Her tendency to act first, ask questions later had often caused her to regret her actions in hindsight. She had not only not asked Joe the questions, she hadn't even allowed him to contact her. She had blocked him at every turn.

It was excruciatingly painful to confront her role in the breakup of their relationship. Would she be making a huge mistake in pursuing a divorce? But how could their marriage continue if Joe didn't love her?

The newly married couple kissed and the guests clapped and cheered and again Juliette was reminded of the brief kiss Joe had given her at their wedding, and the less than enthusiastic applause from the handful of guests, her parents in particular.

After Lucy and Damon's official photos were taken further along on the beach, the mostly informal and relaxed reception was held in the villa's ballroom overlooking the beach.

Juliette got up to dance with three of the other groomsmen to avoid dancing with Joe. She was worried she would betray herself in his arms, reveal things about herself she knew she shouldn't be feeling while she had divorce papers to hand to him. Dance after dance, drink after drink, she worked the room as if she had graduated as star pupil at Social Butterfly school. But inside she was shrivelling up, struggling to cope with pretending to be happy. One of the guests—another cousin of Damon's—was heavily pregnant and every time

Juliette looked at her she felt a hammer-blow of sadness crash over her.

Juliette took yet another glass of champagne off a passing waiter and turned to find Joe standing beside her.

'Is that a good idea?' He nodded towards her glass, his expression brooding.

She arched her brows. 'Since when did you join the Temperance Society?'

He took the glass out of her hand and placed it on a nearby table. 'I think you've had enough.'

'I think you need to back off,' Juliette said, glowering at him. 'Just because you're not having a good time doesn't mean I can't.'

'*Are* you having a good time?' His gaze was as pointed as his tone. But then he released a heavy breath and added with a frown, 'You're pretending, just like I am. But doing a much better job of it than me.'

Some of Juliette's anger faded. She couldn't explain why—it just slumped inside her like a windless sail. 'It's a form of torture, isn't it? Watching other people being happy.'

'*Sì.*'

Juliette tried to read his expression but it was like trying to read a cryptic code. Or maybe it was because her head was starting to pound from all the champagne she'd consumed. Or maybe it was because she knew she was getting closer to the moment when she would hand Joe the divorce papers. She couldn't allow her defences to let her down now. She had come on a mission to get those papers signed. One kiss did not a reconciliation make. She pinched the bridge of her nose and winced. 'I think I need to go to bed. Do you think Lucy and Damon would be offended if I slipped away now before they leave?'

Joe glanced to where the happy couple were dancing cheek to cheek. 'No. I don't think they'll mind. Come on—' he held out his hand '—I'll walk you back to our room.'

Joe led Juliette back to their room. *Their room.* One last night suffering the torture of having her close enough to touch. Close enough to remember the potent magic that brought them together in the first place. Close enough to regret how he had handled every step, every stage of their relationship. Close enough to wonder if there was a chance— a slim chance—she would consider trying again.

The idea crept into his head and looked around for a place to get comfortable, pushing his conscience, his fears, his doubts out of the way. He wasn't imagining the chemistry still between them, was he? It was as strong and pulsing as ever.

Their kiss had proven how strong their connection still was.

How could he forgive himself for not at least exploring the possibility of reconciling?

Joe closed the door of their room but he realised immediately his timing was way off. Not only was there a fold-out bed set up in the sitting room area but Juliette looked tense and on edge. Her teeth chewed at her lip, her eyes not quite meeting his.

'Are you okay?'

She nodded and sat on the sofa and held a scatter cushion against her body like a shield. 'I will be. I just need a glass of water.'

Joe fetched her one and brought it back to where she was sitting. She took the glass from him, guzzled down the water and then handed the glass back. 'Thanks.'

'Another one?'

'Not right now...' She tossed the cushion aside and reached for her phone in her purse and switched it off silent. 'I forgot I promised I'd send my mother a picture of Lucy and Damon.' She clicked the necessary keys and the sound of the message pinging through cyberspace filled the silence. She continued to look at her phone, her forehead wrinkling in a frown. 'Joe?'

'Mmm?'

She lifted her head to look at him with a puzzled

expression. 'This email here that just popped into my inbox. Is it spam? It says you and I have been nominated for some sort of fundraising award. It says we're Fundraising Couple of the Year.' She held the screen up for him to inspect.

Joe leaned down to read the email, and then straightened to take out his phone and clicked on his own emails. He was copied into the same email she had received. What sort of twisted irony was that? *Couple of the Year?* They were no longer a couple. He slipped his phone back in his pocket. 'No, it's not spam. Remember I told you I'd donated on your behalf? And raised funds through various other means. I sent you emails about it but you chose not to read them. There's a fundraising dinner in Paris next month. We've been invited to go and—'

Juliette sprang off the sofa as if one of the springs had poked her. 'Are you out of your mind? I'm not going to Paris with you. It's completely out of the question. Everyone will think we're still together.'

'So, what if they do?'

'We're not together, Joe.' A stubborn edge came into her voice, her grey-blue eyes steely. 'Just because we've shared a room this weekend doesn't mean anything.'

Joe took a deep breath. No way was he going to

that fundraiser without her. It was the perfect opportunity to spend more time with her. This weekend wasn't enough. How could it ever be enough when he wanted her this badly? 'Juliette. This is not about us. It's about helping others who experience what we went through. If we don't show up as a united couple, then how will it look?'

Her expression tightened. 'It will look exactly as it is. We. Are. Separated.' The emphasis on each word was like three punches to his gut. She went over to her tote bag in the corner of the room and pulled out some papers and came back to thrust them at him. 'Here. I've been saving these for now.'

Joe's gaze narrowed as he saw what it was. Legal papers. *Divorce papers.* A pain spread like fire through his chest, searing through flesh, pulverising bone, taking away his breath.

So, his time in limbo was over.

Juliette had already made up her mind. She had come to their friends' wedding with divorce papers for him to sign. It was over. No sequel. No reruns. The End.

A streak of stubbornness steeled his spine and his gaze. Their marriage would end on his say-so, not hers. No way was he signing divorce papers at his best mate's wedding weekend. He took the papers off her and tossed them onto the seat of

the sofa as if they were nothing more than yester-
day's newspaper. 'I'll sign those when I'm good
and ready. Come to Paris with me and then I'll
give you a divorce.'

Her chin came up and her eyes flashed. 'You're
blackmailing me?'

He gave a grating laugh. 'Damn right I am.
What were you thinking, bringing those to your
best friend's wedding? I thought you had more
class.'

She picked up the legal papers and carefully
fed them back inside the envelope. Her movements were calm and controlled but he could see
the effort it cost her. Her jaw was tight, her mouth
pressed flat, her anger a palpable presence in the
room. She put the envelope back in her tote bag
and faced him with fire and ice in her gaze. 'We'll
discuss this again in the morning. I have a headache and don't want to argue with you right now.'

Joe locked his gaze on hers, his own anger stiff-
ening his spine. Anger so thick and throbbing he
could feel it pulsing in his veins like a thousand
pummelling fists. 'You'll hear the same thing from
me in the morning. I will not sign those papers
until I'm good and ready. End of.' He turned and
walked out of the suite and closed the door behind
him as firmly as a punctuation mark.

* * *

Juliette winced as the door shut behind him. She let out a ragged breath. *That went well.* She tugged at the pins holding her hair up and shook her head to loosen the strands. It didn't help her headache, nor did the thought of confronting Joe again with the divorce papers. Why was he being so stubborn and obstructive? Hadn't he said being together again was the last thing he wanted? Or was he interested in a little affair with her until after Paris? She couldn't allow herself to be used in such a way. She wouldn't allow herself to be exposed to more hurt when he failed to support her in the way she wanted. *Needed.* He was all for helping others in their situation, but what about helping her? Supporting her?

When Juliette woke the next morning, after a fitful sleep, she found a note propped up on the bedside table, written in Joe's distinctive handwriting.

See you in Paris,
Joe.

She glanced around the room. His luggage was gone. There was no trace of him in the suite. It was as if he had never been there with her.

Isn't that the truth?

She gritted her teeth and scrunched the note up in a ball and threw it at the nearest wall. 'I'll see you in hell first.'

CHAPTER SEVEN

One month later...

JULIETTE WEIGHED UP the options of informing Joe she would be calling on him at his villa in Positano or showing up unannounced, to hand deliver the divorce papers. She would get those papers signed if it was the last thing she did. She'd had zero contact from him since Lucy and Damon's wedding—not that she had contacted him either. Still seething with anger at the way he had issued her with an ultimatum, and the way he'd left without saying goodbye, it had taken her this past month to feel ready to face him again.

She was *not* going to be controlled by his outrageous demands.

In the end, Juliette decided to just show up at his villa, suspecting if she gave him the heads-up he might find a convenient excuse for not being there. She had heard via Damon that Joe was currently at his luxury villa high in the hills overlooking the Mediterranean ocean, so she was confident it wouldn't be a wasted journey. Besides, she still had a key and, unless he had changed the locks, she would stay there until he returned even if it took a week or two. Those papers needed to be processed and they could only be processed if he signed them.

That was her goal.

Her mission.

Get a divorce. Get on with her life.

But, due to travel delays and her taxi taking several costly—and she thought deliberate—wrong turns, Juliette didn't arrive until late in the evening. Which was deeply annoying, as she hadn't planned on staying longer than the five or ten minutes it would take to get the papers signed. She dismissed the taxi, figuring she would call another one as soon as she was done and then go to the hotel she'd booked online before flying back to London tomorrow.

She was reassured that some lights were on in the villa and pressed the doorbell. No answer. She pressed it again. And again. Still no answer. There was a security camera at the front entrance, so she knew if Joe was inside he could see it was her. Why wasn't he answering the door? And if he wasn't home and one of the household staff was there, why weren't they responding?

It was way too early for Joe to be in bed... although if he had someone with him... Juliette tried to ignore the sharp jab of pain that suddenly assailed her. He had to move on some time. He would definitely do so once their divorce was finalised.

Why was she getting upset about it? It was petty and immature of her. She was over him. She *had* to be.

There was no going back.

Juliette reached in her bag for her key and placed it in the lock, praying he hadn't changed the alarm code, otherwise the security system would screech loud enough to hear in Naples. She opened the door and, wheeling in her overnight bag, stepped inside and closed the door softly behind her.

'Hello?' Her voice echoed through the marble foyer and somewhere further inside the villa she heard something fall over and then Joe's deep voice letting out a filthy curse.

Juliette left her overnight bag at the front door and walked further into the villa. 'Joe?' She went to the smaller of the two sitting rooms, where she could see a pool of soft light shining from the door that was ajar. She pushed the door further open and saw Joe standing near the drink's cabinet with a shot glass of spirits in his hand. The room was in disarray. The sofa scatter cushions were askew, one of them on the floor some distance away as if it had been thrown there. The air was stale as if the windows hadn't been opened in days. Newspapers littered the floor and there was an empty pizza box with traces of topping—olives, capers, mushroom—stuck to the cardboard.

If Joe looked shocked to see her suddenly appear announced at his villa, he didn't show it on his face. He simply raised the glass to his lips, tipped back his head and drained the contents, before wiping the back of his hand across his lips.

'To what do I owe this honour?' His tone was bitter, his eyes bloodshot, his hair tousled, his lean jaw shadowed with at least two days' stubble. His shirt was creased and untucked from his trousers, giving him an unkempt look that was at odds with the man she knew. It was one of the things she secretly admired about him. He took care with his appearance. He wasn't a junk food eater. He didn't drink to excess. He was careful about over-indulging. Unlike her ex, whose idea of a gourmet meal was a deluxe burger at a fast food chain. And who had embarrassed her on more than one occasion by drinking too much and acting inappropriately.

Like *she* could talk after all the champagne she'd drunk at Lucy and Damon's wedding, but still...

Juliette frowned, shocked to find Joe in such a state. 'Are you...drunk?'

He gave a twisted smile that didn't reach his eyes. 'No, but it sounds like fun. Want to join me?' He placed his glass down on the drinks cabinet and reached for the bottle of spirits.

She dropped her tote bag on a nearby chair and came further into the room, stepping over the pizza box and a collection of newspapers. 'I'm not here to party, Joe.' She injected her tone with as much gravity as she could even though it made her sound like the fun police.

He poured a measure of spirits into the glass and she was relieved to see it was only a few millimetres, not centimetres. 'Want one?' He held the glass out to her with a daredevil light in his dark eyes.

'No, thank you.'

'I can open some champagne for you.' His smile had a hint of cruelty about it. 'We could get drunk together and see what happens.'

Juliette pressed her lips together as if she were channelling a starchy schoolmistress. 'That won't be necessary. I don't have anything to celebrate.'

The glint in his gaze hardened to flint. 'Not even my birthday?'

Juliette stared at him for a stunned moment. How could she not have realised? She had never actually celebrated his birthday with him as they hadn't been married long enough. She'd seen it on his passport, though—April the fifth.

But wait... That date rang another bell...

What twist of fate had her coming to visit him on the *exact* date they'd first met? 'I didn't realise until now—we met for the first time on this day. But I thought you said it was the anniversary of your mother's death?'

'*Sì.*' His expression was masked. Stony, cold, emotionless—all except for a shadow lurking at the back of his gaze.

She frowned as she tried to join the dots. 'Your mother died on your *birthday?*'

He put the shot glass down with an audible thud. '*Sì.*'

Her throat was so clogged it felt as if she'd swallowed one of the scatter cushions. 'How old were you?' Her voice quavered with emotion, imagining him as a young child dealing with the loss of his mother. Why hadn't he told her when they were together? Why had he kept such important information about himself a secret? And why hadn't she delved a little more deeply—tried to get to know him better? They hadn't been married long and they hadn't married for the usual reasons, but that didn't absolve her. She hadn't taken the time to understand him, to uncover the enigmatic layers of his personality.

'Thirty-three minutes.' His tone was flat but his eyes were haunted. Black, brooding, bleak.

Juliette's mouth fell open and her heart slipped from its moorings. 'Thirty…? Oh, Joe, you mean she died *having* you?'

He turned away to put the lid back on the bottle of spirits, a frown pulling at his forehead. 'It's why I try to ignore my birthday. There's nothing to celebrate in knowing your birth was responsible for someone's death.'

Juliette came over to him and touched him on the arm to get him to face her. 'I can understand how you, or anyone, would feel like that. But you mustn't blame yourself. It could have been a medical error or—' Even as she said the words, she realised how unfairly she had blamed him for their baby's stillbirth. Guilt was a heavy stone in her belly—crushing, punishing guilt.

He removed her hand from his arm. 'Look, I know you mean well but I'd rather not talk about it right now.' He rubbed a hand down his face, the rasping sound against his stubble loud in the silence. He let out a long breath and added, 'Why are you here? Have you changed your mind about Paris? It's next weekend. Don't forget—no divorce without it.'

The divorce papers could wait. Handing them to him on his birthday seemed a bit crass, considering the circumstances. Besides, her feelings of remorse were so overwhelming she didn't want to do anything she would regret later. She had enough regrets. As for Paris… Would it hurt her to go with him? Maybe it would help both of them find some measure of peace going forward.

'I'm not just here about the divorce. I wanted to come anyway…for another reason.'

Joe took a bottle of water out of the bar fridge and unscrewed the cap, his gaze watchful. 'Which is?'

'Erm…research for my next book.' It was a lie but she could make it true by doing a few sketches while she was here. That was if he hadn't thrown out her art materials. She had taken virtually nothing with her when she'd left. And he hadn't sent any of her things on to her. She couldn't possibly leave him tonight, not on his birthday. At first, she'd thought he was properly drunk, but she realised now he was in a brooding mood and tired. As if he hadn't slept in weeks. And he looked like he'd lost weight—his cheeks were hollow and fine lines ran down either side of his mouth.

He moved past her and sat on one of the sofas, his long legs stretched out in front of him and crossed at the ankles. He took a couple of mouthfuls of water, his gaze tracking back to her as if he couldn't help himself. 'How long do you plan to stay in Italy?'

Juliette sat on the opposite sofa and placed her hands on her thighs. 'I haven't decided. I thought I'd see how I go… It's been a while since I've drawn anything—I might not be able to do it any more…'

Joe took another mouthful of water and then his gaze locked back on hers. 'Where are you staying?' There was a guarded note in his tone.

'I booked a small hotel down near Fornillo Beach.'

His jaw worked for a moment. 'Are you with anyone?'

'No.'

Silence ticked past.

Juliette tucked a strand of hair back behind her ear for something to do with her hands. She felt restless and on edge, uncertain of how to behave around him. Way too tempted to behave in ways that would make a mockery of the legal document in her overnight bag, still on the floor in the foyer. She wished she had the courage to walk behind the sofa where he was seated and massage his tense neck and shoulders like she used to do.

Joe leaned his head back against the sofa cushions and closed his eyes. 'I'll let you see yourself out.'

She was being dismissed.

A wall had come up and she was on the wrong side of it. But something kept her seated on the sofa, something kept her gaze focused on the lines and planes of his face, something breathed life into a dead place deep inside her heart. Juliette felt the stirring in her chest, the slow unfurling of closed wings, the gentle flap of hope coming to life. Hope that their relationship might not be in its last throes but had the potential to rise again.

But better this time.

She hadn't taken the time to get to know him in the past. Her shock pregnancy had propelled them too fast into marriage without the appropriate getting-to-know-you lead-up. And the devastation of losing their baby had blinded her to the things that had worked well in their relationship. Could they possibly build on those things?

'Joe?'

He cracked open one eye. 'What?' His one word, somewhat sharp reply wasn't encouraging but Juliette was starting to realise he was probably feeling uncomfortable with her seeing him in less than ideal circumstances. He felt vulnerable and unguarded and for such a control captain that was anathema.

Juliette glanced in the direction of the kitchen. 'Do you mind if I make myself a cup of tea?'

'Go for it.'

'Do you want one?'

One side of his mouth tilted in a bad boy smile. 'I'm not ready to be a teetotaller.'

'I know you're not drunk. You're only pretending to be.'

He leaned forward to rest his elbows on his thighs and lowered his head into his hands. 'I didn't ask you to come here. I'd rather not have an audience right now.' The *keep away* quality in his tone didn't daunt her. Not now she knew how vulnerable and exposed he felt.

Juliette came over and perched on the arm of the sofa next to him. She raised her hand and began stroking her fingers through the thick strands of his black wavy hair. He gave a low deep groan but didn't push her hand away. Every now and again her fingers would catch on a knot in his hair and she gently untangled it.

After a while, he raised his head from his hands and looked at her with his pitch-black eyes and something slipped sideways in her stomach. 'You should have left five minutes ago.' His voice was so rough it made the hairs on the back of her neck tingle.

Juliette idly ran her finger down the slope of his nose. 'Why should I?'

He grasped her wrist with the steel bracelet of his fingers and her heart gave an excited leap. His fingers were warm, the tensile strength an erotic reminder of other parts of his body that were hot and strong and potent. 'Because I might not let you go.'

Was it the whisky talking? Or was he expressing feelings he had hidden from her in the past?

Juliette used her free hand to stroke his richly stubbled jaw. 'Joe…why didn't you tell me about your mother when we got married? You barely told me anything about yourself. And when I fished for information, you would shut me down or distract me with something else. Or disappear for days on end with work commitments.'

His gaze shifted from hers to stare at her wrist in his grasp on his lap. His other hand came over the top of her captured hand and his index finger traced each of the tendons on the back of her hand. 'There wasn't much to tell. My birth caused my mother's death and my father did his best to raise me but her death was a dark cloud over our relationship.'

'Do you mean he blamed you?'

He gave a lopsided twist of his mouth that wasn't anywhere near a smile. 'Not in so many words. But every year on my birthday since I was old enough to remember, he would take me to the cemetery and make me tidy her grave and put flowers there. I hated going. I found it creepy, to be honest. I put my foot down when I was fifteen and said I wasn't going again. And I haven't. Not once.'

Juliette's heart contracted. She could picture him as a small toddler, not quite understanding why he had to perform such a morbid duty. And then in the years while he was growing up, still being forced to confront the reality of his mother's death and his innocent part in it. So many pennies were dropping in her head she was surprised Joe couldn't hear the loud tinkling. Was that why he had been so distant and aloof at their baby's funeral? He had been almost robotic, hardly saying anything to anyone, not showing any emotion and not comforting Juliette in the way she had needed. Was that why he had never visited their baby's grave? And during Juliette's pregnancy, the further along it went, the further along it went, he had retreated into himself, closed off, distanced himself. Had he been terrified all along that the same thing could happen to her that happened to his mother?

'Oh, Joe…' Tears stung her eyes and she turned

her hand over in his and gripped him tightly. 'I wish I'd known. How terrible that must have been for you as a small child.'

Joe released her hand and rose from the sofa, moving to the other side of the room with his back towards her. 'Why are you really here, Juliette?' His tone had a cold razor-sharp edge. Accusing, cutting, callous.

Juliette swept her tongue over her carpet-dry lips. 'I told you—I'm doing some research for—'

He swung around to face her with a brooding expression. 'You're a terrible liar.' He moved across the room and rummaged amongst some things on the small table near a pile of books. He picked up a pen. 'Got the divorce papers with you?' He clicked the pen open and smiled a savage smile. 'Where do I sign?'

Juliette rose from the sofa and hugged her arms around her middle. 'It's a really dumb idea to sign legal documents when you've been drinking even a small amount of alcohol. I think we should talk about this some other time.'

He clicked the pen on and off several times and she got the feeling it was his way of counting to ten to control his simmering anger. After a moment, he tossed the pen aside and walked past her out of the room, throwing over his shoulder, 'I'll let you see yourself out. I'm sure you haven't forgotten the way.'

Juliette closed her eyes against the sting of his parting words. But there was one thing she was certain of—no way was she leaving tonight. Not until they had chance to talk about things they should have talked about months ago.

Joe had enough trouble resisting Juliette when he was stone cold sober and even though he had only had a couple of shot glasses of whisky he knew it was wise to keep his distance. He was disgusted with himself for indulging in a pity party on his birthday. He mostly tried to ignore the date but this year had brought it all back. The anniversary of the day he'd met Juliette. The amazing night of hot sex he hadn't been able to forget. The amazing night that for once had made him forget what day it was. The amazing night that had cumulated in a pregnancy. A doomed pregnancy, because that was the sort of stuff that happened to him, right? He had a poisonous touch and it was no good thinking it was going to change any time soon. If ever.

He knew why Juliette was here. Those wretched divorce papers. He couldn't put off signing them for ever. English law stated a couple married in England could be granted a no-fault divorce after two years of separation. They had now been separated for sixteen months.

In another eight months they would both be free.

No-fault? Of course there was someone to blame.

Him.

CHAPTER EIGHT

JULIETTE WAITED DOWNSTAIRS until she was sure Joe
had taken himself to bed. She went back out to the
foyer and carried her overnight bag rather than
wheel it, so as not to disturb him. There were several spare bedrooms on the second floor to choose
from. The master bedroom door was closed and in
darkness, so she assumed Joe had settled down for
the night. She toyed with the idea of checking on
him but decided it was best to leave him to sleep
off his devil-may-care mood. She didn't trust herself around him, especially when he was in such
a reckless state of mind. Besides, re-entering the
room they had shared during their short marriage
would test her in ways she wasn't sure she could
handle. Too many images came to mind of her
being in that bed with him, her legs entangled with
his, her body responding to his surging thrusts
with wanton abandon.

She suppressed a delicate shudder and continued on her way to one of the rooms further along the wide carpeted corridor until she came to the closed door of the nursery. She stopped outside, unable to take another step. It was as if a thick glass wall had sprung up in front of her and she could go no further until she glimpsed her baby's room—to see if it was as she had left it.

She had decorated the nursery herself, spending hours in there painting a frieze for the walls, making a mobile for the cot, placing soft toys on the floating shelves she had designed and got made specially. She'd chosen the pink fabric for the curtains with fairies and unicorns on it and made them herself. Every stitch, every brushstroke, every item had been placed there with love. Love for her baby.

They had found out at the twenty weeks scan they were having a little girl. At first, Juliette had wanted to leave it as a surprise but Joe had wanted to know. She understood so much more about him in hindsight—his uneasiness at that and the other appointments she'd managed to drag him to. She'd put his lack of enthusiasm down to the fact the pregnancy wasn't planned, that they weren't in love with each other, that they were only together because of the baby. But now she could see how difficult those appointments must have been for him. How he would be thinking of his mother and how his mother's pregnancy with him had ended in his birth and her death. If only she had known, if only he had told her, maybe their relationship wouldn't have floundered so badly after losing their baby.

Juliette still couldn't say her name out loud. *Emilia.* Once she'd been out in London and a young mother had called out to a small child with the same name. Juliette had to leave the store—she didn't even stay long enough to buy the things she had come for. She couldn't hear that precious name without going to bits.

How would it feel to walk into her nursery?

Or had Joe redecorated the room since she'd left? Had he stripped his villa of any record of her and the baby? The need to know was unbearable, even though she knew by opening the door she would be tearing open an already raw and seeping wound.

She took a deep breath and turned the handle and pushed the door open, reaching for the light switch on the wall. It was like a time capsule. Nothing had changed. The toys with their soft little bodies and sightless eyes were keeping watch over the empty cot. The hand-embroidered quilt was smoothly tucked in, the sheets neatly folded. The cross-stitched sampler she had made was framed above. *Emilia.*

Juliette's throat closed, her heart gave a spasm, her eyes filled. Joe hadn't changed a thing. Everything was the same. Everything. She walked further into the room and touched the mobile over the cot, sending it on a gentle rotation. She didn't have the courage to turn on the nursery rhyme music. There was only so much heartache she could stand.

She brushed at her eyes with the back of her hand, stepping away from the cot to pick up one of the soft toys off the shelf. It was a floppy-eared white rabbit with a pink satin bow. She held it to her face, breathing in the still newish smell, wondering if there would ever be a time when she would be able to think of her baby and not have this aching weight pressing down on her chest.

Juliette put the rabbit back on the shelf and went to the chest of drawers next to the change table. She pulled the first one open and looked at the tiny vests and booties and onesies lying there. She picked up a pair of booties—booties she had knitted herself. She swallowed and put them back and closed the drawer, her eyes burning, chest aching, emotions smashing through her like brutal, punishing waves.

She walked back to the door and turned for one last look at the room. Could there be anything more heartbreaking than an empty nursery, never used?

And then, with a sigh, she switched off the light and softly closed the nursery door behind her.

Juliette went further along the wide corridor to the spare room furthest away from the master bedroom. She opened the door and switched on the light but stopped short when she saw Joe lying face down on the bed. Naked. *Gulp.* He was soundly asleep, his strongly muscled legs splayed across the mattress, his arms resting either side of his head.

She ran her hungry gaze over his toned back and shoulders, feasted on the taut shape of his buttocks, his hair-roughened legs. She came closer, reaching for the throw rug on the foot of the bed, gently easing it out from under his feet and laying it over him to keep him from being cold, even though it wasn't a particularly cool night.

Why was he sleeping in one of the spare rooms? Why not in the master bedroom?

Juliette began to step backwards away from the bed to leave the room when he opened his eyes. He turned over onto his back, the throw rug slipping to barely cover his pelvis. Dark masculine hair arrowed down from his muscle-ridged abdomen, disappearing under the throw rug, but her memory filled in the rest of the picture for her. Hot colour rushed to her cheeks and her pulse flew off the starting blocks and raced and raced and raced.

'I—I'm sorry...' She backed further away from the bed. 'I didn't know you were sleeping in here.'

He sat up and pushed his hand through his sleep-tousled hair. 'I sleep better in this room.' He yawned and threw off the throw rug, stood and stretched, and her female hormones jumped for joy.

Juliette turned her back so quickly she became lightheaded. Or maybe that was because the sight of him naked was enough to make her faint. With desire. 'Could you please cover yourself?' She sounded like a prim spinster from another century but she couldn't look at him without wanting him.

Joe came over to her and placed his hands on the tops of her shoulders. Juliette sucked in a ragged breath, her senses reeling at his closeness. She could feel his body heat—*his naked body heat*—behind her, tempting her to lean back to feel the deliciously hard ridge she was almost certain would be there.

He leaned down to place a kiss just below her left ear and she tilted her head sideways to allow him access, her will to resist evaporating. 'Haven't you heard that saying—*let sleeping dogs lie*?' The soft movement of his lips against her skin, the waft of his warm breath, the deep rough burr of his voice was enough to make her legs fold beneath her like severed marionette strings.

'I told you—I didn't know you were in here. I was looking for somewhere to sleep and—'

He turned her to face him, his eyes sexily hooded and focused on her mouth. His thumb came up and brushed her lower lip, and something deep and low in her belly rolled over. 'Sleep with me.'

It was a command rather than a request and for some reason she was fine with that. More than fine. She didn't want to overthink why she was standing in the circle of his arms with her body burning with lust. But somehow, being back in this house with all the memories it contained shifted something in her—especially now she understood more about him. Things about his personality that made her see him in a totally different light. A light that drew her closer and closer like a storm-tossed dinghy towards the strong, steady glow of a lighthouse. Right now, all she wanted was to be in his arms, to feel the potent power of his body within hers, to feel nothing but passion, lust, longing and have those primal needs satisfied. By him.

Juliette placed her hands around his neck, pressing closer to the hard heat of his body, her body responding with humid heat of its own. She could feel the slick preparation of her inner core, the dew of arousal signalling her readiness, her eagerness, her wantonness. 'Are you telling me or asking me?'

Her voice was just shy of a whisper but still managed to contain a spirited note.

He gave a crooked smile and drew her flush against him. 'Right now, I'd get on my hands and knees and beg if that's what you wanted me to do.'

She stepped up on tiptoe and brought her mouth to just a breath away from his. 'This is what I want you to do.' And then she closed the distance between their lips.

He made a desperate sound at the back of his throat and his arms tightened around her. His lips moved against hers in a series of hot presses, massages, nudges, teases. She opened to the commanding thrust of his tongue, the blatantly erotic movement sending lightning strikes of electricity straight to her core. Flickers and flames of want leapt through her body and she wondered how she had managed to survive so long without this conflagration of the senses. Her body was alive and wanting, aching with the need to have him deep within her.

Joe lifted his mouth off hers and started working on her clothes. 'Let's get rid of these. I want to look at you. All of you.'

Juliette tried to help him but her hands weren't cooperating. Besides, they were already occupied exploring his muscled chest and toned abdomen on her journey down to his erection. She took him in her hand and stroked him the way she knew made him wild for her.

Joe groaned and pulled her hand away. 'Let's get you naked first.' He continued to remove her clothes and each time a slip of fabric fell away from her body she shivered as his glittering gaze ran over her. 'You're so beautiful. So hot. I'm going crazy here.' His fingers struggled with the fastening on her top. 'Damn it. Why do you wear such complicated clothes?'

Juliette laughed and helped him with the fastening, leaving her in nothing but her bra and knickers. His hands cupped her breasts and even through the delicate barrier of lace her flesh leapt at his touch. Her nipples tight, her breasts tingling and sensitive, her inner core aching with need.

Joe placed his hands on her hips, his expression now gravely serious. 'Are you sure about this, *cara*? We can't undo this once it's done.'

Juliette brushed her lips against his. 'Totally sure. I want you. Don't make me wait any longer.'

He brought his mouth down on hers in a firm kiss that spoke of his own escalating need. Their tongues met and tangled, heat flaring between their bodies like an out of control fire. Joe deftly unclipped her bra and it fell to the floor at her feet. His mouth lifted off hers as he slid her knickers down her thighs. She stepped out of them, kicking them aside with one foot, and then moving close to his body again.

He cradled one of her breasts in his hand, his thumb stroking her budded nipple, sending shivers shooting to the core of her being. He brought his mouth down to her breast, his tongue circling her nipple, his teeth gently grazing the sensitive nub and his lips caressing the dark circle of her areola. Tingles coursed through her body, hot tingles and fizzes that sent her senses into a frenzy. Need throbbed and ached between her legs in a pounding rhythm in time with her racing blood.

'You have no idea how long I've ached to do this…' His voice had a ragged quality as one of his hands cupped her mound.

Juliette gasped with delight when he inserted one thick finger into her wet heat. 'Oh, God, I've missed this. I've missed you.' She shuddered from head to foot as his finger caressed her, his expert strokes sending hot streaks of longing down through her pelvis.

He brought his mouth back to hers in a long drugging kiss that made her forget about everything but the sensations coursing through her body. He tasted of salt and a hint of whisky and danger but she was addicted to all of it. Addicted to all of him. The flickering caress of his fingers sent her catapulting into a dizzying flight, spinning her into an abyss where she was conscious of nothing but the exquisite sensations rippling through her.

Juliette gripped his shoulders with her hands. 'Don't let me go. I might not be able to stand upright.'

'I'm not letting you go. I haven't finished with you yet.' His rough tone and strong hands made her insides quiver like an unset jelly.

He walked her to the bed, laying her down and coming down beside her, his dark eyes unashamedly feasting on her body. He trailed a lazy finger from the upper curves of each breast, down her sternum to the tiny shallow cave of her belly button. He spread her thighs and brought his mouth down to the secret heart of her body. She sucked in a breath, heady anticipation for his touch sending another hot shiver down her spine. His tongue tasted her, teased her, tantalised her into another earth-shattering orgasm. It went on and on, sending shudders throughout her flesh until she was breathless and gasping.

Joe placed his hand on her abdomen, his gaze doing a slow appraisal of her body. 'I want you.'

Take me. Take me. Take me.

Juliette panted it under her breath, her heart still hammering in the aftermath of ecstasy. But her body still craved him, it craved his presence deep inside and she reached for him, cupping him in her hand. 'What are you waiting for?' she said.

He eased her hand off his erection. 'I need to get a condom. Don't go anywhere.'

'I won't.' Juliette lay back and watched him hunt for a condom but it was taking too long. Her need for him was throbbing like a tribal drum between her legs—deep, pulsing, insistent.

He opened his wallet and swore, tossing it back down again.

Juliette propped herself up on her elbows. 'What? Don't you have one? What about in the bathroom?'

Joe came back over and leaned down to press a hot hard kiss on her mouth. 'I'll be right back.'

Joe hoped he still had condoms that weren't past their use-by date. Using protection was an issue, irrespective of whether they were officially back together or not. The thought of exposing Juliette to another pregnancy, another terrible loss was out of the question. But what was this…this interlude for Juliette? What was it for him? Just a quick scratch-the-itch-and-regret-it-in-the-morning?

Either way, it was a risk he was prepared to take. He wanted her. He wanted her with an ache so hot and hard and tight it was making him crazy. Making him think beyond tonight. Making him hope they might salvage something from the train wreck of their relationship.

Joe rummaged in the bathroom cupboard off the spare bedroom and found a couple of condoms in his toiletries bag he used when travelling. They had been there for months without him even noticing. But why would he have noticed them? He hadn't been interested in sleeping with anyone since Juliette had left. Not just because he considered he was technically still married, but because he couldn't stomach touching another woman. Being with any woman other than Juliette was repugnant to him. In the past, he'd had his share of casual flings—more than his share. His wealth and status made it easy to pick up casual dates. He had not even thought about it before he'd met Juliette. It was like following a script: drink and/or dinner, dive into bed with an equally enthusiastic and willing partner.

It had worked until it hadn't worked.

He'd met Juliette, they had a one-night stand and whoomph. He hadn't been the same since. He hadn't slept with anyone else since the night he'd met her. Not even when he had no contact with her for three months until she tracked him down to tell him she was carrying his baby. He'd blamed it on his work schedule—he was too busy, travelled too much, was too tired for the chase. All those things might well have been true but he knew deep down it was because sleeping with Juliette had shifted something inside him and he couldn't shift it back. But he would have to find a way, because there were no guarantees she would stay if he offered her a reconciliation.

He had to remember: she'd come here to get the divorce papers signed. Her willingness to sleep with him was probably nothing more than a parting gift. A farewell… Insert coarse swear word. That was all it could be, right? Why was he thinking it could be anything else?

Joe went back to the bedroom to find Juliette lying on her stomach with her chin propped up on her hands. He drank in the smooth curves of her spine and bottom, his lower body twitching with impatience to glide between her legs and thrust home.

'Did you find any?'

He held them up in his fingers. 'Only two, so if you have any ideas of a marathon you'd better hold that thought.'

Something passed over her features and her eyes momentarily slipped out of reach of his. 'What are your plans for the rest of the weekend?' Her tone was casual. Too casual.

Joe came and sat beside her on the bed, placed his hand on her hip and turned her so she was lying on her back. He leaned closer, placing his hands either side of her head, caging her in, his gaze feasting on the sweet globes of her breasts. His groin pounding with feverishly hot blood. 'Shouldn't I be asking *you* that question?'

Her eyes flicked to his mouth. 'I don't know what this is…' She touched her hand to his jaw, grazing her fingers along his stubble. 'I mean… what we're doing…'

'Seems pretty obvious to me, *cara*.' Joe leaned on one elbow and traced his finger around one of her nipples in a lazy circle. 'We're getting it on.'

She pulled her lower lip partway into her mouth, releasing it again, her eyes still troubled. 'Break-up sex? Or…something else?'

It was the million-dollar question Joe didn't have an answer for. He kept his expression casually indifferent when inside he was mentally holding his breath. 'What else could it be? You came here wanting a divorce.'

A small frown pulled at her forehead and her finger brushed over his lower lip. 'I came here determined to get you to sign those papers. It was my goal. My mission…but now…' She gave a tiny sigh and her hand moved to the back of his neck, bringing his head closer. 'I want you to make love to me. I know it's probably wrong or inconsistent of me when I've been waving divorce papers in your face, but it's what I want for now. Just while I'm in Italy.'

A break-up fling with his soon-to-be ex-wife.

But Joe wanted her any way he could have her. 'I want you to stay until after the Paris fundraiser.' He knew he was taking a risk using such a commanding tone but did it anyway.

Her eyes flicked to his mouth and her tongue darted out to lick her lower lip, tightening the ache in his groin another unbearable notch. 'Okay. I'll go with you to Paris.'

'Good. But as long as we're both clear on what this actually is.'

Was *he* clear? The only clarity he had was that this felt right. Having her here in his arms. The trouble was…how was he going to let her go when it was time for her to leave? Or could he dare to hope she would stay? But that would mean resuming their marriage and look at what a rubbish job he'd done of it the first time around.

'I want you, Joe.' Her voice was as soft as her touch.

'I want you so badly.' Joe covered her mouth and lost himself in the hot, sweet temptation of her lips. His tongue met hers and a lightning bolt of lust shot through his groin. He gathered her in his arms, their legs tangling in a way that was achingly familiar and yet no less thrilling. It was like discovering her body for the first time—the dips and slopes and contours, the honeyed secret of her centre, the taste of her mouth and the feel of her breath mingling intimately with his.

He left her mouth to kiss his way down the scented hollows of her neck, over the delicate scaffold of her collarbone, all the way to her breasts. He took each nipple in his mouth, rolling his tongue over the tightly budded flesh, his blood thrumming with excitement. Her soft breathless groans, the arching of her spine, the folding out of her knees to welcome him made his heartrate spike. No one could turn him on like her. No one got him so worked up and ready to explode. No one.

He slipped on a condom and, putting a hand under her left hip to tilt her towards him, entered her with a deep thrust that made the hairs on his scalp stand up and a shudder ripple through him. She welcomed him with a gasp and began moving with him, her smooth slim legs in a sexy tangle with his. It was too hard for him to slow down as he'd planned. Too hard to resist the magnetic pull of her silken body. He thrust and thrust, his blood racing like rocket fuel through his veins, his skin tingling from head to foot. He placed his hand between their rocking bodies to caress her.

She threw her head back, writhing and whimpering as her orgasm took her away and carried him with her. The tight rolling spasms of her body sent him flying into the stratosphere. He buried his face into the side of her neck and groaned and shuddered and shook as his release powered through him in pulses and waves and ripples, taking him to a place beyond thought. Beyond the ugly divorce word, beyond the lonely emptiness of a future without her in it.

Beyond anything but mindless, magical bliss.

CHAPTER NINE

JULIETTE WOKE TO find herself spooned in Joe's arms. One of his legs was flung over hers, his head buried against the back of her neck, where she could feel his deep and even breaths stirring her hair. One of his hands was resting on her ribcage and he murmured something unintelligible and glided it up to cup her breast. She shivered with longing, her inner core contracting with the muscle memory of their passionate lovemaking during the night.

He groaned and sighed like a satisfied lion and propped himself up, turning her so she was on her back, his dark gaze smouldering. He brushed her hair back from her forehead with a touch so gentle it made something in her chest spring open. 'So here we are. The morning after the night before.' His tone was playful but she sensed an undercurrent of gravity.

She pushed back his hair from his forehead with her splayed fingers. 'You probably need to find a better way of getting through your birthday without drinking on your own or having one-night stands with strangers.'

He circled her mouth with a lazy finger, his gaze suddenly inscrutable. 'Is that what last night was? A one-night stand with a stranger?'

Juliette lowered her hand to his jaw, stroking his lean cheek with a feather-light touch. 'You don't feel like a stranger to me now. Not after we talked about…stuff.'

A frown flickered on his forehead and his gaze became wary. 'Is that why you slept with me? Out of pity?'

She pulled her hand from his face and jerked her chin back in shock. 'How could you think that? I wanted to make love with you. I practically begged you to.'

He placed a firm hand on the flank of her thigh to keep her moving further away, the heat of his touch sending a fizzing current to her core. 'There's probably a lot of stuff I should have told you before. But I try to forget about how I came into the world. I don't like thinking about it, much less talking about it.'

Juliette slid her hand back to rest against his cheek, her thumb stroking back and forth over his prickly skin. 'It must be awful to not look forward to your birthday. It must have been so painful growing up without a mother, especially feeling so guilty about how you lost her. But it wasn't your fault. Your father should've made that absolutely clear.'

His gaze flickered with shadows, as if he was leafing through his childhood memories like fanning through the pages of a thick book. 'He was grieving for a long time. I didn't understand that until I was much older. He was like a zombie walking through life. He was only a young man. My mother was the love of his life—they met in primary school. They married at twenty-one.' His mouth twisted and his eyes briefly squeezed shut as if he was experiencing the most excruciating pain. 'And she was dead at twenty-two. She didn't get to live the life she'd planned. She didn't get to reach her potential, to do the things most people dream of doing.' He swallowed and continued in a strained tone, 'I hated going to visit her grave. I felt sick to my stomach, because I knew I was the one who put her there. Who robbed her of everything: the man she loved, the future she'd dreamed of, the family life she longed for. I took it all away from her.'

Juliette blinked back tears. 'Oh, Joe, I wish I'd known all that before. I feel so annoyed at myself for not pressing you to tell me more about yourself. Is that why you found my pregnancy so unsettling? I sensed you were staying away longer and longer, the further along the pregnancy went.'

He took one of her hands and brought it up to his chest, holding it against the steady thump of his heart. 'I wanted to support you—that's why I married you, to provide for you and the baby. But when I saw your belly growing bigger each week, a vague panic set in and I could only quell it by distracting myself with work. I don't think I was entirely conscious of it at the time—why I was feeling like that. I just felt compelled to work as hard as I could. But I see how you would've read that as something else.'

Juliette swallowed a knot of emotion in her throat. 'When you got to the delivery suite... I thought you looked relieved... I hated you at that moment. I couldn't believe you were being so brutally insensitive.'

A flash of pain went through his eyes and his fingers on her hand tightened. 'I was relieved. Relieved you hadn't died.' His voice sounded rough around the edges, raw and uneven. 'I didn't think about the baby at that point. All I could think on my way into that room was, *Has it happened again? Have I killed my mother and now my wife?*'

Juliette bit down on her lower lip until she was

sure it would draw blood. She couldn't believe how blind she had been. How blinkered she'd been to think he hadn't cared about her and their child. She pulled her hand out of his so she could hug him around the neck. She rested her cheek on his chest, her throat so tight it was aching. 'I've made so many mistakes. I'm sorry for misjudging you.'

Joe rested his chin on the top of her head and stroked her hair with his hand. 'We've both made mistakes.' His voice was a low, deep rumble against her ear. 'I guess the thing to do now is not make any more.'

Was *this* a mistake? Lying in his arms, wanting him with a need so strong it throbbed deep in her core. A need that made a mockery of the divorce papers she had brought with her. Joe hadn't said anything about loving her. And nor had she to him. She still wasn't sure how to describe her feelings for him. They had been under layers of bitterness and anger and grief and were only now rising to the surface. One thing she did know for sure—they didn't feel anything like the 'love' she'd thought she'd felt for her ex. They felt strong and lasting, healing and hopeful.

How long Juliette wanted to stay with Joe was not so easy for her to acknowledge—even to herself. She'd only booked her hotel for one night, as she'd planned to fly back to England once the divorce papers were signed. But spending the night with Joe and finding out so much more about his background made her reluctant to rush off home without spending a bit more time with him. To answer some important questions that were niggling at her conscience.

She felt foolish and immature for being so intransigent in Corfu about going to Paris with him, but was it too soon to jump back into their relationship? Was it too soon to hope he would grow to love her as she was growing to love him? Or maybe she had always loved him. From the moment they'd met she had felt something shift inside her. The connection they'd formed had rocked her to the core and not just because of the pregnancy and its tragic outcome. Her misplaced anger towards him had covered up her true feelings. Feelings that had sprouted at that first meeting but had been poisoned and almost destroyed by the tragedy of losing their little baby.

'I know you're busy with work but I can hang out here and sketch and relax by the pool until we go to Paris. I'll try not to get in your way.'

One side of his mouth lifted, his gaze gleaming with unmistakable desire. 'You can get in my way all you like.' He traced her mouth with a lazy finger. 'The more the better.'

Juliette shivered at his tingling touch. 'You don't mind me being here?'

'Not at all.' And his mouth came down and confirmed it.

Juliette woke later that morning to find the bed empty beside her. She glanced at the clock beside the bed and was a little surprised she had slept in for so long. How could it be nine in the morning? She couldn't remember the last time she had slept so soundly. Her nights were usually disturbed by restlessness and sleeplessness, rumination and regret.

She threw off the bedcovers and slipped on a bathrobe. *Joe's bathrobe*. She breathed in the scent of him, her senses whirling, her belly fluttering, her heart swelling as she recalled his exquisite lovemaking during the night.

How could she regret last night? It was impossible. She felt close to Joe in a way she had never expected to feel. Knowing more about his heartbreaking background had softened her anger towards him and directed it more at herself. Her own grief had blinded her to the reality of his. Didn't the untouched nursery demonstrate that? He hadn't changed a thing in that beautiful room. Last night, he had shown her with his lips and hands and body how much he'd missed her.

Juliette walked out of the bedroom to head downstairs, where she could hear Joe moving about in the kitchen. But as she was passing the door to the master bedroom she had previously shared with him, she stopped and reached for the door knob. Why did he no longer sleep there? What had motivated him to occupy one of the spare bedrooms instead? She opened the door and, leaving the door open behind her, walked further into the room.

Memories floated towards her, stirring her emotions into a way she hadn't expected. She walked past the king-sized bed where she had spent so many nights wrapped in his arms, when he'd come home from his work trips. She opened the door of the walk-in wardrobe and found her clothes still hanging there as if she had never left. She could even pick up a faint trace of her signature perfume. She came out of the wardrobe and entered the en suite bathroom. Some of the cosmetics and toiletries she hadn't bothered to take with her were on the marble counter and in the cupboards under the twin basins.

Surely he could have got one of his housekeepers to remove her belongings? Why hadn't he? Or had Joe been *expecting* her to return?

Juliette frowned and came out of the bathroom to find Joe standing in the open doorway of the bedroom, carrying a tray with tea and toast and preserves. His expression was hard to read. On the surface he looked relaxed and open but she could sense an inner tension.

'I was just bringing you breakfast in bed.'

'Why didn't you get rid of my things?'

He came further into the room and placed the tray on the bedside table. He straightened to face her. 'I figured if you wanted them you would've taken them with you when you left or asked me to send them to you.'

Juliette searched his unreadable gaze. 'Were you always expecting me to come back?'

Something flickered at the back of his eyes and his mouth took on a rueful twist. 'No. I had given up on that score.' His tone contained a flat note of bleakness.

She sat on the edge of the bed and looked up at him. 'Joe…why don't you use this room any more?'

He ran a hand around his shirt collar as if the fabric was prickling him. 'I told you last night—I sleep better in the other room.'

'But why?'

Joe released a harsh-sounding breath. 'For God's sake, do I need to spell it out?'

Juliette kept her gaze trained on his. 'Yes, I'm afraid you do.'

He drew in another breath but this time released

it less forcefully. He sat down beside her and took one of her hands in his. His fingers wrapping around hers in a protective cloak. 'Every time I came in here was another reminder of how I'd let you down. I couldn't be in here without thinking about you. It was easier not to come in here at all.'

Juliette lifted her hand to his cleanly shaven jaw. 'Is that why you left the nursery as I left it?'

A flash of pain went through his gaze. 'I can't even bear to say her name, much less go in there and be reminded of her.' His voice was raw with suppressed emotion, his jaw tightening against the cup of her palm.

Tears sprouted in her eyes. 'Oh, Joe, I can't say her name either. Some days, I can't even think it without falling to bits.'

Joe brought his hand to her face, blotting her tears with the pad of his thumb. His eyes were dry but pained. 'My whole career has been based on fixing things that are broken. Finding why things that shouldn't have failed, failed. But I couldn't fix any of this for us.'

Juliette put her arms around him and laid her head on his chest. 'I'm glad we're able to be so honest with each other now. It helps me to know I'm not the only one who feels so undone by what's happened.'

His hand stroked the back of her head in gently

soothing strokes that made the last of the armour around her heart melt away. 'I wish I'd been there to support you better. There's so much I would like to have done differently.' His deep voice rumbled against her cheek—full of low, deep chords of regret and self-recrimination.

'It might have been different if we had known each other better at the time,' Juliette said, glancing up at him. 'I mean, if we'd had a normal period of dating before we married. I feel like I'm only getting to know you now.' When it was too late. Or was it?

He glanced at the tea tray with a wry expression. 'I'm trying to decide whether to feed you breakfast or give you a kiss first.'

Juliette linked her arms around his neck and smiled. 'Just one kiss?'

His eyes smouldered and he gathered her closer. 'Why stop at one?'

And he didn't.

A couple of days before the Paris trip, Joe came in to the morning room where Juliette was sketching. He had been on a lengthy Skype call in his study. 'Sorry that took so long,' he said, leaning down to press a kiss to the top of her head. 'Hey, it's great to see you sketching again.' He picked up one of her earlier sketches—one of him sleeping—and frowned. 'I look so relaxed.' He put the sketch back down.

Juliette swivelled on her chair to look up at him. Something in his expression sent off a distracted vibe. A subtle distance in his gaze. A slight disturbance in his tone.

'Is everything okay? Has something come up with work?'

'I've been thinking about this Paris thing.'

Juliette straightened in her seat, unsure what to make of his expression. 'You still want me to go...don't you?'

'I shouldn't have pressured you into going. I can go alone if you don't feel up to being social.'

Juliette rose from her chair and wrapped her arms around her middle, uncertain of what to make of his seeming reluctance to have her accompany him. Was he wary of being out in public with her in case people read more into their relationship than was true? After all, they weren't officially reconciled. They were having a break-up fling. Did he want to keep their involvement with each other out of the press? Or was there some other reason?

She turned her back to him and stared at the view of the ocean below the steep slopes, with their collection of old and luxury villas and the vivid splashes of colour and greenery. 'Are you worried I might say or do something I shouldn't? That I might disgrace you in some way?'

Joe came over to her and placed his hands on the top of her tense shoulders. He turned her around to face him, his expression etched in lines of concern. 'No. I'm worried people will make you feel uncomfortable. You know how it works at these gatherings. You get stuck next to someone who wants to know every detail about your life or tell you every detail of theirs.' He made a husky, clearing his throat sound and added, 'I know it's a fundraiser for stillbirth research and counselling services but people can still ask intrusive questions. I don't want you to be hurt by someone asking you about things you'd rather not talk about.'

Juliette's heart gave a funny little flutter-spasm.

He was concerned about her. He wanted to protect her.

She had done her usual jumping to conclusions by thinking he was somehow ashamed of her, worried she might drink too much and humiliate him. But it was nothing to do with any of that.

He genuinely cared about her.

She put her hands on his chest, her lower body flush against his. 'I've avoided a lot of social events for exactly that reason. What if someone asks me if I have any children? Or plan to try again? What am I supposed to say? Am I even allowed to call myself a mother when I didn't give birth to a live baby?'

Joe framed her face in his hands, his gaze tender as it meshed with hers. 'You will always be Emilia's mother. No one can take that away from you. No one.'

Tears stung her eyes and a lump formed in her throat. 'Y-you said her name...'

Joe stroked his thumbs across each of her cheeks in a slow soothing motion. 'Maybe some time in the future it won't hurt so much to say it. To think of her.'

'Maybe...' Juliette sighed and leaned her cheek against his chest. 'They say time is a great healer, but how *much* time?'

'As long as it takes, I guess.'

There was a small silence, broken only by the sound of his hand stroking the back of her head and their quiet breathing.

It was an enormous comfort to her that he felt the same sense of loss. She had unfairly assumed he was less affected because he hadn't been the one to carry the baby, to physically give birth, and that he hadn't been there to witness the birth. But she realised now his expression of grief was different from hers.

Not wrong, but different.

Juliette lifted her head off his chest and looked

up at him. 'I can't avoid social events for ever. I want to go with you. It's important to support such valuable fundraising.'

A small smile flicked up the corners of his mouth and illuminated his gaze. 'We could make a long weekend of it. How does that sound?'

She linked her arms around his neck and smiled. 'It sounds wonderful. I haven't been to Paris for years.'

He pressed a kiss to her upturned mouth. 'How remiss of me not to have taken you before now.'

Juliette played with the ends of his hair that brushed his collar. But she was conscious of a small grey cloud of unease creeping closer. Paris. The city of love. Had he taken anyone else in the past? She wasn't aware she was frowning until Joe inched up her chin and smoothed the crease away from her forehead with a gentle finger.

'What's wrong, *mio piccolo?*'

Juliette forced a smile but it fell a little short of the mark. 'I guess you've been to Paris heaps and heaps of times with lots of other…people…' She couldn't bring herself to say the word *lovers*—the pang of jealousy was too intense.

His eyes softened and he drew her closer with one hand resting in the dip of her spine, the other gliding to the sensitive nape of her neck. 'You have no need to feel jealous, *cara.*'

Juliette slipped out of his hold and pretended an interest in straightening her sketches on the table. 'I'm not jealous. I know you've been to lots of places with lots of different people.'

'But none of them have been my wife.'

My wife. The words sounded so…so permanent. But they hadn't decided anything permanent about their relationship. They had discussed a lot of issues, yes. And grown closer in so many new ways. But Juliette knew there would be other issues to discuss. Difficult, painful issues—whether or not to have another child, for instance. That was one of the questions she most dreaded. For months and months since the loss of her baby, she couldn't bear the thought of trying again. Going through another pregnancy with fear and dread on board as well as a baby. A baby there was no guarantee she would deliver alive.

Juliette held onto the back of one of the chairs and glanced down at her ring finger. The vacant space seemed to mock her. He referred to her as his wife but there had been no renewed promises. No official reconciliation. No renewed commitment. No declaration of love.

She brought her gaze back to his. 'Have you told anyone we're…?' She left the sentence hanging, not sure how to describe their relationship. A fling sounded so tawdry. An affair even worse.

'No. Have you?'

She pressed her lips together and released her grip on the chair, using one hand to sweep her hair back over one shoulder. 'I didn't think it was necessary…under the circumstances.'

'Precisely.' Something about the delivery of the word was jarring. Discordant. Like the wrong note played during a musical performance.

Juliette ran the tip of her tongue over her lower lip. 'It would be silly to get people's hopes up. Lucy and Damon, for instance.' *Not to mention her own hopes*.

'But what if the fundraiser draws a lot of press attention? Aren't people going to assume we're back together permanently?'

The ensuing silence was too long. Why wasn't he asking her to come back to him for ever? Why wasn't he dismissing her concerns with a declaration of love?

'There isn't a law about divorcing couples attending a social function together.' Joe's voice sounded tight. Constricted. 'If anything, it will demonstrate how civilised we're being about the whole damn thing.'

She studied his tense features for a moment, wondering if he was having second thoughts about their divorce. But, if so, why hadn't he said anything? 'Joe…?'

He scraped a hand through his hair and released a rough sigh. 'The press will probably make a big thing of it, but that's to be expected. I'll try and shield you as much as possible.'

Juliette approached him, touching him on the forearm. 'I want to be with you.' She couldn't think of anything she wanted more. Not just the Paris trip but with him all the time. For ever. Was she a fool for hoping he would agree to a reconciliation? Maybe the Paris trip would cement their relationship—take it to a new level that would make him realise they had a chance to make it.

The tension in his face relaxed slightly and he cupped her face in his hands. His eyes searched hers as if he was looking for something he'd lost and hoped desperately to find again. 'The dinner is only for a couple of hours. We can spend the rest of the time doing our own thing.'

She linked her arms around his neck and pressed closer. 'I can't wait.'

CHAPTER TEN

THEY ARRIVED IN Paris on Friday afternoon and once they had settled into their luxury hotel Joe suggested they go shopping.

'Shopping?' Juliette looked at him in wary surprise. 'But I don't need anything.'

'How about a new outfit for tomorrow night?' He wanted to spoil her. To make this weekend as special for her as he could. To make this weekend last for as long as he could.

'I brought one with me. You don't have to waste money buying me expensive—'

'I insist, *cara*.'

Something flickered across her features. A tightening. A guardedness. 'Are you concerned I won't dress appropriately?'

Joe mentally kicked himself. He should know by now how proud and sensitive she was. He took her by the hands and brought her close to his body.

'You always look amazing in whatever you wear. Indulge me, *tesoro*. Let me spoil you this weekend.'

Her gaze slipped to the open collar of his shirt, her teeth sinking into her lower lip. 'I feel guilty about all the money you're spending. This hotel, first class airfares, designer clothes.'

He tipped up her face to meet her gaze. 'Don't you think you're worth it?'

Her eyes swam with doubt. 'It's not about that...'

'Then what is it about?'

Her teeth did another nibble of her lip and she slipped out of his hold. 'We're not exactly acting like a soon-to-be-divorced couple, are we?'

'I wasn't aware there was a strict protocol we had to follow.' Joe couldn't remove the note of bitterness from his tone. The divorce word was becoming worse to him than the birthday and funeral words. Every time he heard it, his heart stopped and his gut clenched like a fist.

Juliette turned to pick up her silk scarf from where she had left it on the bed. She looped it around her neck and turned back to face him. 'It feels wrong, taking gifts off you when we're not—'

'Does it feel wrong sleeping with me?'

Her expression faltered for a moment. 'No.' Her cheeks pooled with a tinge of pink and her gaze drifted to his mouth. 'It doesn't feel wrong at all.' Her voice was a few decibels shy of a whisper. 'But I can't help feeling it should.' A frown pulled at her forehead as if she was trying to solve a deeply puzzling mystery.

Joe placed his hands on her hips, his body responding to her closeness with a hot rush of blood to his groin. 'It would only be wrong if one of us didn't want to. Or if one of us was involved with someone else. But, for now, we're involved with each other.'

Her mouth flickered with a vestige of a smile. 'Right.' She took a serrated breath and released it. 'For now.' She said the two words as if she was underlining them.

'If you're not okay with that, then you need to tell me.'

Her grey-blue eyes were clear and still as a lake but he sensed a disturbance just below the surface. 'I'm okay with it.' Her tone was confident, assured. Her smile a little too bright to be believed.

Joe reached for one of her hands and brought it up to his mouth. He pressed his lips to her bent knuckles, holding her gaze with his. 'Then let's make the most of it.'

A couple of hours later, Juliette felt as if she had stepped into Cinderella's shoes. Joe took her to various designer stores, where he proceeded to buy her not one, but several gorgeous outfits. She tried not to think about the money he was spending or why he was spending it on her. It was wonderful to be spoilt like a princess and wonderful to be in his company, walking hand in hand along the streets as if they were just like any other couple.

'Time for a coffee?' Joe said when they came across a street café.

'Lovely.' Juliette sat opposite him and took in the surroundings while they waited for the waiter to arrive. The leafy trees along the footpath created a canopy of dappled shade. The afternoon was mild with a light breeze that every now and again set the leaves above them into a shivery dance that sounded like thousands of pieces of tinsel. In the distance she could see the ancient cathedral of Notre Dame in various stages of repair after the devastating fire that had threatened the entire structure. It reminded her of her relationship with Joe—the savage fire of loss had ripped through their lives and left them both scarred shells of themselves. But maybe this time together would rebuild the framework of their marriage, making it stronger and more resistant to damage.

The waiter took their order and within a short time an espresso was placed in front of Joe and tea and a buttery croissant set in front of Juliette.

She was conscious of Joe's gaze resting on her as she broke off pieces of the croissant. She glanced at him and held up a portion. 'Want some?'

He shook his head, his smile indulgent, and he patted his rock-hard abdomen. 'No, thanks. I have to think of my figure.'

Juliette laughed and put the piece of croissant back on her plate. 'Now you're making me feel guilty.'

There was a small silence.

'I've missed hearing your laugh.' He brought his cup up to his mouth, taking a sip without his gaze leaving her face.

Juliette could feel a light blush heating her cheeks. 'I can't remember the last time I laughed.' She sighed and added, 'It seems like a lifetime ago.'

He put his cup back on its saucer and reached for her hand across the table. His fingers gently squeezed hers, his expression sombre as he looked down at their joined hands. 'I think I was probably five or six years old when I first heard my father laugh. A proper laugh, I mean.' His thumb stroked the empty space on her ring finger. 'I asked him about it once. He said he felt guilty about being happy.' His eyes met hers. 'Like he was betraying my mother's memory.'

Juliette placed her other hand on top of his. 'It

must have been so hard growing up without your mother. Mine drives me crazy at times but I can't imagine not having her in my life.'

His mouth flickered with a smile touched by sadness. 'I could mostly put it out of my mind but now and again something would remind me I wasn't like the other kids at school. Lots of them were in single parent families but mostly it was from divorce or separation, not the death of a parent. Parent-teacher interviews were difficult, and on Mother's Day, when the teacher got us to make cards, I made one for my *nonna* instead.'

'Were you close to your *nonna*?'

'I adored her. She was a widow herself so she understood what my father was going through but she died when I was nine.' His mouth twisted. 'I never met my mother's parents. They refused to have anything to do with my father. They weren't keen on him as a son-in-law in the first place, so you can imagine how they felt once she died. They blamed him for her death. I'm sure it didn't help his grieving process.'

Juliette's heart ached for what he had been through. So much sadness. So much loss. So much grief. Somehow it made what she had been through a little easier to bear. Just a little. 'I don't know how you coped with all that sadness. Did things improve at all once your dad remarried?'

'Yes and no.' Joe released her hand and picked up his coffee cup, cradling it baseball mitt style in one hand. 'My father was certainly happier. And my stepmother was nice enough but it was hard for her bringing up someone else's kid. A kid she had no history with, who she suddenly had to mother when she married my father. When they had two kids together, I felt even more of an outsider.' He lifted his cup to his lips and drained the contents, placing it back down on the saucer. 'And when my father died my stepmother no longer had to pretend to play happy blended families any more.'

If only he had told her this in the past. If only she had understood the trauma and sadness that had shaped his personality—the grief that had robbed him of a normal childhood and made him so cautious about relationships.

Juliette pushed her plate to one side and touched his hand where it was resting on the table. 'I wish I'd known more about your background when we first met.'

His eyes met hers, his fingers wrapping around hers in a gentle hold. 'I can't remember the last time I told anyone about any of this. It's not something I like talking about. Plenty of people have it much worse than I did.'

'Yes, but we were married and I should've understood you better.' She frowned and looked down at their joined hands. His wedding ring was a reminder that she was the one to leave their marriage, not him. Would he remove it once their divorce was finalised? Her stomach pitched at the thought of him being with someone else. She swallowed a tight lump and continued, 'I should've made more of an effort.'

Joe leaned forward and stroked a lazy finger down the curve of her cheek. 'None of this is your fault. You had your own stuff going on with your ex.'

Juliette sat back in her chair with a little thump and folded her arms and frowned. 'I wish you'd stop mentioning my ex. I don't even think I was truly in love with Harvey. I think I only continued with the relationship as long as I did as it seemed to please my parents.'

He studied her for a long moment. 'Were they pleased when we broke up?'

Juliette unfolded her arms and slumped her shoulders on a sigh. 'No. If anything, they thought I was being impulsive and letting my emotions overshadow everything. But I shut them down pretty quickly and they've said nothing since.'

'One could hardly blame you for being emotional, given the circumstances.' His tone was a disarming blend of gruffness and tenderness.

Juliette lowered her gaze, leaned forward and

pushed a piece of croissant around her plate with her finger. 'I don't see much of them these days. They're always so busy with work. I know their careers are important to them but it always makes me feel I'm way down on their list of priorities.' She sighed and added, 'I wonder if it will change when they retire. *If* they retire, that is.'

There was a long silence.

Juliette chanced a glance at him but he was looking into the distance as if his thoughts had been pulled elsewhere. It gave her a moment to study his features—the frown of concentration, the sharply intelligent gaze, the chiselled jaw with its peppered regrowth, the sculptured contours of his mouth. Her belly flip-flopped when she thought about his mouth on hers, the silken thrust of his tongue, the heat and fire of his kiss.

He stirred his coffee even though she knew he didn't take sugar, his gaze focused on the tiny whirlpool he created in his cup. 'Some people live to work—others work to live.'

Juliette shifted uncomfortably in her chair. 'I suppose you think that makes me sound like a spoilt brat, insisting on being the centre of my parents' world.'

His gaze met hers. 'I don't think that at all. It can be difficult when our caregivers don't meet our expectations. Sometimes it's down to circumstances, other times to personality.'

Another silence ticked past.

Juliette shifted her gaze to the left of his. 'I was a change of life baby. An accident. A mistake.'

His expression clouded. 'Surely they didn't say they didn't want you?'

Juliette chewed the side of her lip. 'No. Never—it's just a feeling I've had over the years. Having a child at their stage of life must have been an inconvenience. My brothers were eighteen and twenty. I spent a lot of time with nannies and babysitters and, of course, boarding school, which I hated. I think that's why I never did that well at school. I disengaged out of emotional distress.'

He touched her hand where it was resting on the table. 'Don't be fooled into thinking a bunch of letters after your name makes you smart. You are an intelligent and hugely talented artist.'

Juliette hoped her creative drive would come back stronger than before but it had taken such a blow with the death of her baby. Her motivation had been totally crushed and was only now flickering into life. 'Thanks.'

He smiled and waved a hand at her teacup. 'Would you like a refill?'

'No. I'm done.' She pushed back her chair while

he gathered the array of shopping bags around his chair.

He paid the bill and within a short time they were on their way back to the hotel. Once they arrived, Joe handed the porter the bags and accompanied Juliette to the private lift to the penthouse.

'Why don't you have a bit of a rest before dinner?' he said as the lift arrived at their suite. 'I have a couple of things to see to.'

Juliette tried to ignore the little stab of disappointment that jabbed her. 'Will you be long?'

He leaned down to press a light kiss to her lips. 'Not long at all.'

Joe walked the streets of Paris, ruminating on how he had approached life's challenges. Juliette's comment about her parents always working had struck a chord with him. Ever since he was a young child, he had thrown himself into tasks, study, work, to escape the shadows of his childhood. The loss that had defined him since he'd taken his first breath. Being successful, wealthy and hard-working had given him a framework for his life that had never let him down until he'd met Juliette.

But now he could feel the foundations of his personality undergoing a change, like a fine crack running through concrete. A gradual destabilisation of his identity as a man who needed no one.

Who kept himself emotionally separate, distant. Safe.

But the more time he spent with Juliette, the wider the cracks grew, allowing him to envisage the sort of man he could be if he was able to let go of the past. A man who could love and be loved in return. A man who would no longer need to keep his emotions locked down. A man who could embrace his vulnerabilities and face whatever life threw at him with emotional courage instead of cowardice.

His feelings for Juliette were something he had tried so hard to ignore. And he'd been damn good at it so far. So good he'd convinced himself not to beg her to come back to him when she'd left. So good he'd not revealed things to her he should have revealed while they were together. Things that might well have made a difference if he hadn't been so determined to hold himself apart, as he had done with every other relationship, both intimate and otherwise.

But now his feelings were tiptoeing out of their hiding place, their tentative footsteps leaving soft little impressions on his heart that felt almost painful.

He looked down at the wedding ring on his finger, the symbol of his commitment. A commitment he wasn't entirely sure Juliette wanted from him any more. She had made no commitment other than to spend the next few days with him before she went back to London.

Could he dare to hope to change her mind?

Juliette had showered and dressed and was putting the finishing touches to her make-up in preparation for the dinner when Joe returned to their hotel. She met his eyes in the mirror of the dressing table. 'You're cutting it fine. Isn't the dinner at seven-thirty?'

He gave a crooked smile. 'It won't take me long to get ready.' He came up behind her and, slipping one hand inside his jacket pocket, retrieved a rectangular jewellery box. 'I found something for you when I was out walking.'

Juliette turned on the stool and raised her brows. 'Found? Like on the footpath?' She gave him a mock frown and waggled a reproving finger at him. 'You've been spending money on me again.'

He handed her the box. 'And why shouldn't I spoil you?' He leaned down to press a light kiss to the top of her head. 'Mmm... You smell beautiful.'

Juliette lifted her face to meet his gaze. 'It's the same perfume I've always worn.'

His fingers brushed beneath her chin in an idle movement, his eyes dark and lustrous. 'I know. I smelt it everywhere in the house after you left.' His mouth turned down at the corners as if the mention of that time caused him pain. He glanced at the jewellery box in her hands. 'Go on. Open it.'

Juliette looked down at the box and ran her fingertip over the gold embossed designer label on the black velvet lid. She prised open the lid and gasped when she saw a glittering diamond on a gold chain as fine as a thread and two matching diamond droplet earrings.

'Oh, Joe, they're gorgeous.' She could only imagine how much they'd cost. It was the sort of jewellery designer where one didn't shop if one needed to see a price tag before considering purchasing anything.

'Here. Let me put the necklace on you.' His voice had a gruff edge, his expression hard to read.

She handed him the box and turned so she was facing the mirror again, watching him carefully remove the diamond from its plush white velvet bed. She shivered when his hands brushed the sensitive skin of her neck as he fastened the diamond in place. He handed her the earrings one at a time for her to insert into her earlobes. Then he rested his hands on her shoulders and met her eyes in the mirror.

'You look stunning.'

Juliette touched the diamond with her fingers, the earrings glinting like stars when she turned her head from side to side. 'I hope I don't lose one of them.'

He gave a grim smile that wasn't really a smile. 'There are worse things to lose, *cara*.' His deep tone echoed with a sadness that was almost palpable.

She placed one of her hands over one of his, pressing down on it in an I-know-what-you-mean gesture. Her throat thickened, her chest tightened, her eyes glistened. 'You'd better get dressed. It's almost time to leave.'

He looked as if he was about to say something—his brows moved closer together and his mouth opened as if in preparation to speak—but then seemed to change his mind. He gave her shoulders one last squeeze and turned away to get ready for the dinner.

The fundraising dinner was held in the ballroom of a private mansion within walking distance of their hotel. By the time Juliette and Joe arrived, the guests were making their way to their allotted tables after having drinks and finger food in the foyer. The room was decorated with simple and elegant arrangements of flowers and pastel-coloured paper rosettes and ribbons rather than less environment-friendly balloons.

Joe seemed to know many of the guests and introduced her to several people on the way to their place at the huge table but she found it hard to remember all their names. She smiled and shook hands with everyone, quietly wondering if any of them knew the circumstances about her and Joe's marriage.

Juliette was seated next to Joe, with a woman on her left in her mid to late forties called Marisa, who was on the board of directors for the charity.

'I'm so pleased to finally meet you,' Marisa said with a warm smile. She glanced covertly towards Joe but he was talking to the man next to him and added in a lower tone, 'We so appreciate what you and Joe have done for our charity. It's really lovely too that you could make it here with him.'

'Oh, well, it was really Joe who did all the fund-raising. I'm afraid I had little to do with that at all.'

Marisa placed a gentle hand on Juliette's arm, her expression full of compassion. 'You don't have to explain. What you two went through is enough to tear apart any young couple. I should know. I had a stillbirth in between my first and third child. It was horrendous. I think of him every single day. We called him Alexandre.'

Juliette looked into the other woman's now shimmering hazel gaze and for the first time in months felt less alone and isolated. 'I'm so sorry.'

Marisa's mouth twisted. 'He would have been

ten years old last month. You never really get over it. You carry it with you. I was lucky I already had a child. I'm not sure I would have been game enough to try again if I hadn't. But I'm so glad I did. My two girls are my biggest joy.'

Juliette swallowed a tight lump in her throat. 'How soon did you…try again?' Her voice was as tentative as her thoughts on the subject of having another baby. It was something she had been thinking about ever since she'd walked into the nursery. The thoughts were mostly at the back of her mind, but lately they were creeping closer and closer. Close enough for her to imagine cradling a beautiful baby in her arms.

A live baby.

Joe's baby.

'Months and months,' Marisa said. 'I could barely look at my husband without bursting into floods of tears. But I'd always wanted a family and Henri did too. We decided it would probably help us heal if we tried again. And it worked. It doesn't mean I don't still grieve. I do, and badly at times, and so does Henri. But the thing that helped Henri and me was setting up this foundation a couple of years after we lost Alexandre. Joe's contribution has been invaluable. It's meant we can do further important research as well as adding to our counselling services. It was so very kind and generous

of him, when he was going through such a difficult time himself.'

Guilt rained down on Juliette anew. Joe might
not have visited their daughter's grave but he had
done what he could to stop such a tragedy from
happening to others. Instead of trying to understand things from his point of view, she had pushed
him away, rejected him, marched out of his life
instead of sharing the burden of grief with him—
without allowing him time to process his feelings,
which were just as valid as hers.

'He's…a very kind and generous person,' she
said, her heart so full of love for Joe she found it
hard to take her next breath. Love that had grown
from the moment she'd met him. The first kiss,
the first night together—the night where she had
given herself to him so wholeheartedly. The night
that had bound them together with a subsequent
tragedy. Could they move past it?

Marisa gently squeezed Juliette's hand where it
was resting on her lap. 'You'll know when it's the
right time to try again. You'll probably always feel
worried during any subsequent pregnancy—that's
entirely natural and unfortunately unavoidable.
But the sheer joy of holding your baby at the end
is worth it. There's really nothing like it.'

Juliette squeezed the other woman's hand in return. 'Thank you for sharing your experience with

me. I've found it so hard to talk to anyone about it. Some people in my life think I should have moved on by now.'

'Not Joe, though?' Marisa frowned.

'No, not Joe.' Juliette sighed and continued. 'I've been so hard on him. I was so caught up in how I was feeling that I didn't realise he was feeling the same, only expressing it a different way.'

Marisa nodded in empathy. 'Tell me about it. I often was so angry at Henri for the most ridiculous things until I realised it was misplaced grief masquerading as anger. I could handle feeling angry. What I couldn't handle was feeling profound gut-wrenching, inescapable grief. But eventually we worked through it and are stronger and closer for it.'

Stronger and closer for it.

Juliette mulled over that phrase as the more formal part of the dinner commenced. The award was finally announced and Joe led Juliette up to the podium. Press cameras went off and later a journalist requested an interview. Joe spoke briefly about the foundation and skilfully steered the journalist away from their personal situation. It made Juliette all the more uncertain of what he ultimately wanted from her. A fling before they divorced—or did he want her to stay with him for ever?

Stronger and closer.

Would those words one day define her and Joe? The desire to heal was so strong in her now. Stronger than her anger, which seemed to have dissipated like fog under the hopeful beam of sunshine. And she realised now a part of that healing included fulfilling her dream of having a family. Of being part of a loving partnership with her husband, raising children in a house where love and acceptance and nurture were at the forefront at all times.

Time was reputed to be a great healer, but wasn't love the best healer of all?

CHAPTER ELEVEN

THEY WALKED BACK to their hotel in silence. Juliette had so many questions to ask, so many doubts to address, so many hopes to allow the freedom to grow. When they were back in their room she turned to look at him.

'Joe? I wish I'd known about your work with the foundation. It means so much to me that you've tried to help so many others like us. I'm sorry I blocked contact with you.'

He slipped off his jacket and hung it loosely over the back of a chair. His mouth was pressed flat for a moment and his eyes looked pained. 'I was almost glad you blocked me. I was worried about upsetting you. Every time we talk about the baby...' his throat rose and fell and his voice grew raspy '... I see what it does to you. It hurts you.'

Tears sprouted in her eyes and she went to him, wrapping her arms around his waist. 'But it hurts me more *not* to talk about her. Losing Emilia will always upset me. It's normal and unavoidable. We suffered a terrible loss. But I want to move on as best I can and that includes talking about how we're feeling and when we're feeling it.'

Joe cupped one side of her face, his other hand going to rest on her hip. His gaze held hers in a tender lock that made her heart contract. 'I felt so powerless and frustrated our baby died. Giving to the foundation was the only thing I could think to do to remove some of that powerlessness. I figured by donating and raising large sums of money for research it would stop it happening to someone else. It helped me process my grief by actually doing something positive. I didn't want to be like my father, who was so prostrated by grief it took years for him to come out of it.'

Juliette stroked his jaw, leaning into his strong frame, her body responding to his closeness with its usual leap of excitement. 'I think you're amazing to have done that. It shows the wonderful man you are. Generous and kind and compassionate.'

He brought his head down so his mouth was just above hers. 'Don't make me out to be too much of a hero, *tesoro*. I have many failings.'

Juliette linked her arms around his neck. 'Kiss me, Joe. Make love to me.'

He drew her closer, his arms a strong band

around her body, his mouth coming down on hers in a kiss that was soft and yet deeply passionate. Sensations swept through her body— hot, urgent sensations that made her weak at the knees. He lifted her in his arms, carrying her as if she weighed little more than a child, and took her through to the bedroom. He lowered her feet to the floor in front of him, his hands already setting to work on her clothes. Juliette got to work on his and within moments they were both naked and lying, limbs entwined, on the bed.

Joe's mouth came down on hers, firmer this time, his tongue entering her mouth to tease hers into erotic play. Molten heat pooled in her core, need pulsating deep in her feminine flesh. His mouth moved from her lips to explore the soft skin below her ear, his tongue flickering against her sensitive flesh until she writhed with pleasure. He went lower to her décolletage, tracing the fine structure of her collarbone and down to the gentle swell of her breasts. The action of his mouth and tongue evoked tingles and prickles and needles of pleasure through her breasts. Her nipples tightened, her spine melted, her need escalated.

His hand went to her hip, gliding to her bottom to tilt her towards him. '*Dio mio*, I want you so much.' His voice was a low, deep, agonised groan. He kissed her again, his tongue tangoing with hers until she was mindless with desire. He lifted his mouth off hers and rolled away to get a condom.

Juliette thought of telling him not to bother, that perhaps they should try for another baby instead of using protection. But she decided to keep that conversation for another time. A time when she had a better understanding of how he felt about her. He had never said he loved her. But she knew deep in her bones he cared about her. Cared more than he was probably willing to admit. And wasn't she a bit the same? She hadn't declared her love for him. Not yet.

Joe applied a condom and came back to gather her close. His eyes were so dark with desire they looked densely black. 'I'm glad you came with me to Paris.'

Juliette pressed a soft kiss to his mouth. 'I'm glad I came too. And, speaking of coming…' She hooked one leg over his and gave him a come-hither look.

'Leave it with me.' He smiled a sexy smile and brought his mouth back down to hers. 'I'll see what I can do.'

During the night Joe reached again for Juliette, his arms gathering her close to his body. She made a soft murmuring sound and nestled closer, her head resting on his chest right where his heart beat a steady rhythm—but not for much longer. He could feel the quick uptake of his pulse as his body responded to her silky skin, her smooth limbs, the soft waft of her warm breath. The scent of her filled his nostrils, the glide of one of her hands against his thigh making his breath catch. His groin swelled, heated, burned at the thought of her touching him. Desire rolling through him in ever-increasing waves.

The moonlight coming in through the window cast her body in silvery light, making her look like an angel that had flown from heaven and lain down beside him. *Heaven* just about summed up what it felt like to hold her. To make love to her. To feel her body enclose his, to feel her respond to him hadn't lessened his desire but rather fed it, nurtured it, expanded it.

Her hand crept ever closer until she was encircling him with her fingers. 'Are you awake?' Her voice was a whisper that made his flesh tingle all over.

He smothered a groan as his body throbbed under her touch. 'I am now.'

She glanced up at him with shining eyes, a cheeky smile curving her lips. 'Do you want me to stop touching you?'

Joe felt like he would *die* if she stopped touching him. He rolled her over to her back and leaned over her with his weight propped on his elbows. 'How about I touch you to even this up a bit?'

He cupped one of her breasts, rolling his thumb over her nipple, watching her response play out on her features, in the catch of her breath, the parting of her lips, her gaze flicking to his mouth. His hand went down from her breast to the tiny cave of her belly button and then beyond.

'Oh…' Juliette gave a breathless gasp, her legs folding outwards to welcome his touch. *'Oh…'*

Joe moved down her body, using his lips and tongue to bring forth her earth-shattering response—a response that never failed to thrill him. Making love with her was on another scale from anything he had experienced before. A scale he had never reached with anyone else. Her response to him touched him at the centre of his being. Making him *feel* every movement of her body, every stroke and glide of her fingers, every soft press of her mouth, as if his body's nerves had been tuned to another setting. A higher, richer, more pleasurable setting.

Juliette flopped back down against the pillows, her face flushed, her eyes bright as gemstones. 'I'm not letting you get away with that without a payback.'

'Is that a promise?'

She smiled and scrambled to a sitting position,

pushing him down so he was on his back. 'What do you think?' She straddled him and slid down his body until her mouth was close to his erection.

He sucked in a rasping breath. 'I can't think right now.'

'Then don't. Just feel.' And when she closed her mouth over him that was all he could do. He was reduced to sensations so powerful, so all-consuming, he thought he would lose consciousness. The teasing suction of her mouth, the sexy glide and the kittenish licks of her tongue made him fly into a vortex of mind-blowing, senses-spinning ecstasy.

He came back to earth with a deep sigh of contentment and brought her down so she was lying on top of him, her legs entangled with his. He stroked the length of her spine in slow movements, enjoying the press of her breasts against his chest, the beat of her heart against his, her hair tickling him where it cascaded over him like a mermaid's.

He listened to the gradual slowing of her breathing, felt her body gradually melt into full relaxation as she drifted off to sleep.

A long time later he too closed his eyes but it was a long time before he went to sleep…

On Monday morning Joe woke a little later than was normal for him. He turned to reach for Juliette but the space beside him in the bed was vacant. For a brief moment panic gripped him in the chest like a claw—a sudden, savage claw that reminded him of all the mornings he had woken without her beside him. But then the sound of her moving about in the bathroom relaxed his tense muscles like the injection of a prophylactic drug. Relief swept through him in deep calming waves.

After spending the weekend wandering around the city of Paris hand in hand, they were flying back to Italy this afternoon. He could not remember a time when he had felt such a deep sense of hope. Hope that their relationship had a chance to be restored, regenerated, renewed. But while Juliette had initially agreed to stay a couple of weeks, she hadn't said anything about staying longer. He *wanted* her to stay longer. He wanted to resume their marriage. To start afresh. To build on the new understanding they had now after spending time together.

Juliette came out of the bathroom already showered and dressed. 'Good morning, sleepyhead.' Her smile was as bright as the sunshine pouring through the window and his breath caught in the middle of his chest.

'Yes, well, you did wear me out a little last night.' Joe smiled and tossed off the bedcovers and slipped on a bathrobe in case he was tempted to take her back to bed and cause them to miss their flight.

She gave an answering smile but something about a look in her eyes gave him pause. 'Joe?'

He came over to her and ran his hands down from her upper arms to her wrists, gently encircling them with his fingers. 'What's on your mind, *cara*?'

She drew most of her lower lip into her mouth, holding it there for a beat before releasing it. 'You know how I said we should be honest about our feelings? Well, I don't want to go ahead with the divorce.'

Joe pulled her to him in a tight hug, his relief so immense it flooded his being. 'I don't want that either. I want you to stay with me.' His voice was hoarse with suppressed emotion, his heart thudding with joy. 'We'll start afresh. Go on a proper honeymoon this time. We can even renew our vows if that's what you'd like.'

She leaned back to look up at him, her grey-blue eyes clear. 'Why, though? Why do you want our marriage to continue?'

Joe could feel a ripple of unease slithering down his spinal column. 'You know why. We're good together. We understand each other better now.'

Her eyes drifted to his mouth. 'Joe, a marriage

is not just about good sex.' Her gaze came back up to his. Direct. Determined. 'I love you.'

Joe knew he should fill the silence with the answer of those overused words but his mouth dried, his chest tightened. He had never said those words to anyone. Not even his father or Nonna. He had showed it in other ways, but saying those words out loud would trigger something primal in him. Born out of some kind of primitive desire to keep himself free of deep emotional entanglements.

'*Cara*, you know I care about you.' Somehow he spoke past the stricture in his throat.

Her expression faltered, hurt flickering through her gaze, her mouth sagging at the corners. 'I don't want you just to care. I want you to love me. And I want us to try for another baby. I'm ready now. Please say you're ready too?'

Something in his chest gave way as if his heart had suddenly been dislodged, like an industrial crane losing its heavy load. He couldn't take a new breath. He became lightheaded, disoriented. Panic beat in his chest as if fists were punching inside his heart to escape.

Another baby... Another pregnancy... Another nine months of worry. Of dread. Of anguish.

Joe let his hands drop from around her wrists and stepped back, fighting for air. For composure.

For safety. 'Whoa there. That's not something I can even think about. Not right now.'

She frowned, her mouth opening and closing as if she couldn't think of what to say. Then she took a steadying breath. 'Joe.' Her tone was level, calm, rational. 'I know you're worried about what might happen to me or the baby or both. I suspect most husbands would feel that way if they were asked, especially after going through what we went through. But we'll have the best of medical care and we can only hope this time the baby will be okay.'

Joe shoved a hand through his hair, his brain reeling so much it felt as if his skull would fracture. 'I'm not ready to discuss this.'

'But, if we're to stay together, we have to discuss difficult things as they come up. Isn't that what we did wrong in the past? We pushed it under the carpet instead of airing it up front.'

He moved to the other side of the room, unable to get his thoughts out of their frenetic maelstrom. It was like a tornado of terror inside his head. 'I'm not willing to discuss it. No way.'

Her eyes widened, her cheeks losing colour. 'No way...*ever*?'

He scrubbed a hand down his face, his chest still so tight he could barely inflate his lungs. His gut prickled with anxiety, his head pounded, his brain log-jammed. He wanted a reconciliation. It was all he wanted—to have Juliette back in his life. But to go through the stress of another pregnancy, knowing it could end like the last one, would be a step too far. A dangerous, frightening step that made everything in him freeze in panic.

'Look, I'm happy to resume our marriage—really happy—but having another baby is out of the question. I just can't face it. I'm sorry.'

Her brow was furrowed with confusion. 'But I thought you cared about me? I even thought maybe you…loved me, even though you seem unwilling to say the words.'

Love was something Joe had never expected to feel with any intensity. Whenever he felt the stirring of emotions he couldn't handle he blocked them. Deadened them. Denied them. He let out a long breath. 'I told you—I care about you.'

She moved further away, crossing her arms over her body. 'But you're not in love with me.' Her tone was flat, resigned, dull.

Joe swallowed against another tight knot in his throat. 'I've never felt like this with anyone else, but as to whether it's the love you want, well, I can't guarantee it is.'

She met his gaze with a steady focus that was unnerving. Unnerving because he felt a horrible sense of history about to repeat itself. 'I spent so much of my childhood wondering if I was loved like my brothers were loved. Never quite feeling I made the grade. I didn't seem to tick the boxes my parents wanted ticked. I always seemed to disappoint them. It made me feel like an outsider in my own family. I don't want to live like that in our marriage. I want to be on an equal footing with you. A true partnership where we share everything openly and honestly.'

What could he say that he hadn't already said? He *was* being honest with her. Brutally so.

'I'm sorry you feel that way about your family. It's tough feeling like you don't belong. I get that. But a marriage like ours could be successful without the idealised, overly romanticised version of love you're talking about.'

Juliette ran her tongue over her lips and continued, her voice becoming husky. 'I could probably cope with you not being in love with me. I knew when you married me you didn't love me that way. But I want another baby at some point. It doesn't have to be right now. But how can we have a future together if you won't even discuss it?'

'Of course we have a future together,' Joe said, struggling to contain his poise. 'Hasn't the last week proved that? We're in a much better place than we ever were before. We know each other so much better and—'

'I know all that but it's not enough.' Her slim shoulders went back as if she was drawing on some inner strength to get her point across. 'I want a family, Joe. I want to be a mother so badly. I can't guarantee it will happen, especially given what happened last time, but I still want to try.'

The punching panic in his chest was at a manic stage, like a boxer going for the knockout blow. Desperate to get out of the ring no matter what.

'Look, children obviously are an important part of many people's lives. But we've been down this road and it nearly destroyed us. Why not quit while we're ahead? We can have a great life. Travel to anywhere at any time and never want for anything.'

Her eyes dulled, her expression faded, her throat tightened over a swallow. 'You never wanted her, did you? You never wanted a baby in the first place. That's why you don't want another one now. It's not part of your life plan. It never has been.'

'That's not true. I wanted our child as much as you did—'

'Tell me honestly. Do you *ever* want another child?'

The silence clawed at his guts, tore at his heart like talons.

'I'm not sure I can answer that.' He finally found his voice.

Her grey-blue eyes became glacial ponds, her expression hardening like a hoar frost. 'I think I get it now. Sorry for being so slow on the uptake.' Her tone chilled the temperature in the room to an arctic level. 'The problem as I see it is you don't want to have a baby with *me*. I'm the problem.' She batted her hand against her chest for emphasis. 'It's *me*.'

'That's not true,' Joe said, scrambling for a way out of this wretched conversation. He was in quicksand and sinking. He could feel it dragging him down, down, down. He had seen whole buildings crumple and disappear into sinkholes. Could there be a bigger, blacker pit of despair for him to fall in? To lose her again? Not once, but twice?

But…another baby?

No. No. No. He couldn't go through it again.

Her spine straightened, her gaze determined. 'If you don't want to be the father of my child, then it's time for us to say goodbye.'

No! The word was a silent scream inside his head. A siren of blind panic. A high-pitched screech of fear that made his blood run cold. But, rather than voice it out loud, Joe curled his lip instead, determined not to show how undone he really was. He would climb out of that damn sinkhole and take control. He *had* to. He'd done it before. He would do it again.

'Blackmail doesn't suit you, Juliette. And you should know by now, I'm not the sort of man to respond to it.'

Her small neat chin came up and her eyes glittered with defiance. 'Then we are at an impasse.'

'Don't be ridiculous,' he began.

'I'm not being ridiculous—I'm being realistic,' Juliette said. 'What would be the point in continuing our marriage if one of us isn't getting what we want? Who never gets what they want? I'd end up resenting you. Hating you for denying me the family I want so much.'

Joe strode over to her but refrained from touching her. If he touched her, he would agree to anything. He couldn't risk it. He needed time to process what she was demanding. It was too much for him to handle when they had only been back together a matter of days.

'There's always compromise in relationships,' he said, shocked at how calm and collected he sounded when on the inside he was collapsing like a badly constructed office tower. The very foundation of his being was under threat. He was teetering over an abyss of uncertainty, dread, uncontrollable danger.

Juliette met his gaze with a level stare. 'I know all about compromise. I'm the one who made all the adjustments, fitting into your life when we first got married. But I'm not prepared to compromise on this. It's not fair to ask me to. If you loved me, you would understand how important this is for me.'

'Then maybe I don't love you.'

One side of Joe's brain was shouting, *What are you saying?* The other was saying, *You're safe, for now.*

She flinched as if he had slapped her and, right at that moment, he had never hated himself more. But wasn't it better this way? He had always known on a cellular level he would not be enough for her. He wasn't good for her. He had all but destroyed her life by getting involved with her in the first place.

The blame for so much suffering was at his door.

'Then I think that's all that needs to be said.' Her voice was almost as calm and indifferent as his but he could see how much he had disappointed her. It was in every nuance of her face—the tight lips, the creased brow, the dullness of her grey-blue gaze as if a light had been turned off inside her. 'I won't be returning to Italy with you this afternoon. I'll fly straight home to London.'

Home to London.

The words were vicious hammer blows to his heart. But he had no way of defending himself without bringing more pain and uncertainty into both of their lives.

Juliette turned away and began packing her things into her weekend bag.

Stop her. Stop her. Stop her. Tell her the truth. Tell her how you feel about her. Don't let her leave like this.

But Joe did the opposite. He walked calmly, silently into the bathroom, and when he returned a few minutes later she was gone.

Later, Juliette could barely recall how she got to the airport and on a plane to London without displaying the devastation she felt. It was as if she had split herself into two people—one was calm and logical and rational, able to call a taxi, pay the driver and board a plane without a qualm. The other was a broken, shattered shell, limping through the steps to get her to somewhere safe where she could address her terrible wounds.

Joe didn't want another child.

Joe didn't love her.

He had never loved her.

She had fooled herself into believing otherwise. She had constructed a dream landscape where the pain of the past would fade into the background, not quite going away but no longer causing the distress it once had. A landscape where the birth of another baby would bind her and Joe in the joys of parenthood, their marriage thriving instead of dying. How could she have been so naïve? How could she have allowed herself to think they had a future when he was unable—*unwilling*—to love her?

Was there something wrong with her that she was destined to crave a love she couldn't have?

Juliette had always doubted her parents' love for her, seeing it as conditional rather than unconditional. She had thought Harvey, her ex, had loved her and had foolishly believed it when he'd said the words so often and so volubly. But that had also been a lie.

She huddled into her seat on the plane and looked listlessly out of the window at the clouds drifting by. Her heart ached as if an invisible corkscrew were driving through it on the way to her backbone.

So, it was finally over.

Her marriage to Joe Allegranza was dead.

Unsalvageable.

Could there be anything crueller than to dangle hope in front of her and then snatch it away? Every kiss, every touch, every time they made love, she felt that he loved her. How could she have been so misguided? So fanciful? So deluded?

It was time now to move on and forge a new path for herself. A new future.

Juliette's heart gave another painful spasm.

Without Joe...

Joe spent the first week after Juliette left throwing himself into work, largely helped by a bridge collapse in northern Spain. Fixing other people's problems was the only way to distract himself from his own unfixable ones. But, as much as he found his work rewarding and challenging in equal measure, he began to realise it no longer filled the gaping chasm Juliette had left behind. His work was like temporary scaffolding holding up a compromised building.

He was the compromised building, constructed from materials that were now seriously out of date.

Stoicism, self-reliance, a fierce desire for control, emotional lockdown, an isolationist mindset were no longer materials in a man's life that worked, if indeed they ever had. They were destroying him like termites in the foundations, quietly, secretly, stealthily destabilising and destroying the man he had the potential to be.

But where to start to fix such deep-seated faults?

He knew exactly where—at the beginning.

* * *

Joe's mother's grave was sadly neglected and a deep sense of shame washed over him as he knelt down beside it and pulled out the weeds from around her plot. He placed the flowers he'd brought with him in the stone vase and sat back on his heels to read the words engraved on the marble headstone.

Giovanna Giulia Allegranza
A loving wife and mother
Missed for ever

He had no knowledge, no physical memory of his mother, and yet he sensed how much she must have loved him. He was touched that his father had insisted the word 'mother' was included on her headstone even though she hadn't regained consciousness to hold Joe in her arms. Why hadn't he noticed that before now? All those times his father had dragged him to the graveyard, Joe had stood sullenly to one side as his father tended the grave with tears pouring down his face. It had repulsed Joe, made him feel his father was weak and unable to control his emotions, that he had loved his wife *too* much.

Why had he adopted such toxic notions about manhood? Why had he denied himself for all these years the full breadth and depth of his humanity? The ability to feel and express deep emotion, the ability to willingly relinquish control over things that couldn't be controlled in any case, to acknowledge his grief over the loss of his baby daughter.

And the deep and abiding love he felt for Juliette.

Why else was he struggling to make sense of his future without her? The emptiness she'd left behind could not be filled with work. No amount of work could ever do that. He loved her with a love so strong it seeped into every cell of his body like the pouring of concrete on a building site. His love was the solid, dependable, unshakable platform on which they could plan a future.

Joe stood from his mother's grave and glanced at some of the other headstones nearby. There were numerous stories of love inscribed there. Old love, young love and everything in between. Life had no guarantees. You could be lucky to live to ninety. Some, like tiny Emilia, didn't survive the nine months of pregnancy. Some didn't survive childhood or middle age, and yet others lived long lives and still they were grieved. Grief had no age limit. It was a human response to loving someone. It didn't matter how old they were—they were missed when they were gone.

Like he missed his baby daughter...

Pain gripped him in the chest and he blinked against the moisture at the back of his eyes. Could he do it? Could he visit that tiny grave and confront the raw grief that threatened to overwhelm him?

CHAPTER TWELVE

JULIETTE WAS IDLY sketching at her flat in London, her mind preoccupied with missing Joe. She hadn't heard anything from him since she'd left him in Paris. Not that she'd expected to—they had both said all that needed to be said. But when the doorbell rang her heart leapt and her deadened hopes took a gasp of air.

She opened the door and her shoulders slumped on a sigh. 'Oh…hi, Mum…' Her tone was jaded and unwelcoming even though she was craving company. Any company to distract herself from her misery.

'Have I come at a bad time?' her mother, Claudia, asked.

Juliette forced a weak smile. 'Of course not. I was just doing some drawing…' She led the way into the kitchen, where she had set up her art materials.

Claudia glanced at the sketches. 'So, you're working again?'

'Sort of.' Juliette shuffled the papers into a neat pile. 'I'm thinking about doing a children's book on loss. I thought it might help when kids lose a parent or someone close to them. Or even a pet.'

'That's a wonderful idea,' Claudia said, pulling out a chair to sit. She waited a beat before adding, 'Did you get the divorce papers signed?'

Juliette hadn't told her mother about the few days in Italy with Joe or the weekend in Paris, and realised now how awkward it was going to be to fill in the gaps.

She slid into the seat opposite. 'Mum…for a time I was considering going back to him. We caught up at Lucy and Damon's wedding and then I went to see him in Positano. I stayed for over a week and I really thought we had a chance to make things work. I found out his mother died having him. How tragic is that? I realised while I was there that I love him. I know this might sound a bit fanciful to someone as rational and logical as you, but I think I fell in love with him the moment I met him. And I want to have another baby but he's adamantly against even discussing it. I can't compromise on that. I know there's no guarantee I won't have another stillbirth but I want to try for another child.'

Claudia reached for Juliette's hand and gave it a motherly squeeze. 'Sweetie, falling in love like that doesn't sound fanciful at all.' She sighed and continued. 'I might appear rational and logical to you, but I'm not always like that on the inside. I fell in love with your father in much the same way. It was so sudden and I always felt as if I had to prove myself to his parents—your grandparents—to justify him marrying me.'

'Really? But I thought Nanna and Pop adored you.'

Claudia's smile was rueful. 'They did, eventually, but mostly because I did everything I could to please and impress them. My Masters and PhD? That was my way of showing them I was as intelligent and capable as their son. Worthy of him.' Her expression faltered. 'When I got pregnant with you, I had just enrolled in my PhD. I couldn't bear the thought of dropping out and yet I was so torn about you. There were times when I hated leaving you with the nanny and other times when I couldn't wait to get away so I could concentrate on my work. I couldn't seem to win, no matter what I did. And, being an older mother, well, I just didn't have the energy and drive I had with your brothers.'

'Oh, Mum…' Juliette stood and came around

to give her mother a hug around the shoulders. 'I think most mothers feel like they can't win.'

Claudia turned in her chair and grasped Juliette's hands. 'I wish I could make you happy, sweetie. The last few months have been so tough on you. But, given what you told me just now about Joe, it's been terribly tough on him too. He must have been beside himself the whole pregnancy. No wonder he doesn't want to go through that again. He wouldn't want to risk losing you.'

Juliette slipped her hands out of her mother's hold. 'He doesn't love me, Mum. He told me he cares about me. That's not enough. I want him to love me.'

Claudia frowned. 'Sweetie, are you sure he doesn't love you? One thing my long career in science has taught me is to look closely at the evidence. Examine every bit of data, check and double check and keep a rational perspective. Men aren't always good at expressing their emotions. Sometimes they don't even recognise what they're feeling. Years of being taught to suppress how they feel makes it hard for them to open up when they need to.'

Could her mother be right? But why had Joe let her leave both times without asking her to stay? Why hadn't he called or texted?

He'd left her stranded in a vacuum.

'I don't know...' Juliette sighed. 'I sometimes thought he loved me. He's so generous and kind. But he hasn't contacted me since I left him in Paris. Not even a text or phone call. If he cared about me, wouldn't he want to contact me?'

'We always expect people to respond to a situation the way *we* would respond, but each of us has their own way of doing things, their own framework or lens to view things through,' Claudia said. 'Joe strikes me as someone who takes his time to think about things before he acts. He's just taking longer than you would like.'

'But what if you're wrong?'

Claudia gave a soft smile. 'Look at the evidence, sweetie. It's all you can go on for now.'

After her mother left, Juliette bought flowers from her local florist and drove to the graveyard where Emilia was interned in a small village outside London. It never got any easier and it was particularly difficult on cold wet days when the miserable sky above felt as if it was pressing down on Juliette with the sole intent to crush her. But the sun was out today and birds were twittering in the shrubs and gardens that fringed the cemetery. The roses were in full bloom and the rich clove and slightly peppery scent wafted on the gentle breeze.

Juliette walked towards her daughter's grave

but, as she got closer, something caught her eye. There was a new teddy bear with a pink tulle tutu sitting propped up next to the marble headstone. She bent down and read the card that was attached to the teddy bear.

To my darling Emilia
Love you for ever, mio piccolo
Rest in peace
Papà

It was Joe's distinctive handwriting. The combination of English and Italian a touching tribute to their baby girl's heritage. He'd been here. Recently. He had visited Emilia's grave for the first time since her funeral.

He was here in England.

Juliette turned and scanned the graveyard for any sign of him but, apart from an older couple standing next to a grave several metres away, there was no one else here. Her shoulders slumped and she turned back to Emilia's grave and set about placing the flowers in the vase. Just because he was in England didn't mean he would seek her out.

What else could he say other than what he'd already said?

Then maybe I don't love you.

How those words had tortured her, bruised her,

destroyed her hopes like noxious poison sprayed on a delicate bloom.

Juliette drove back to her flat in London with a heavy heart. It was all very well for her scientifically trained mother to insist she look at the evidence, but how could she survive another rejection?

She turned the corner into her street and saw a tall figure standing at her front door. Her heart gave a leap, her pulse thudded, her hopes rose. She tried to play it cool by parking her car with casual ease, even though she felt like banging and crashing into the cars before and aft in her haste to get to Joe.

She walked towards him with her expression as blank as she could muster but she could do nothing about the way her heart was thumping. 'Hello.' How stiff and formal she sounded. As if she was addressing a cold caller or doorstep salesperson.

'Can we talk inside?' Joe's tone was gruff, his expression guarded.

'Okay.' She unlocked her door and went in, conscious of his tall frame coming in behind her. The scent of his aftershave teasing her senses, her body reacting automatically. Wanting to touch him. Be held by him. Loved by him.

The door closed behind him and silence descended. A weighted silence.

'I saw the teddy bear,' Juliette said.

'Yes, I went there this morning.' He swallowed and continued in a fractured tone. '*Cara*, can you ever forgive me for how I've handled everything? I'm ashamed of how blind I've been to how I feel about you.'

Juliette took a steadying breath, not quite ready to let her hopes run free. 'How do you feel about me?'

He smiled and took her hands in his. 'My darling, I love you. I think I've loved you since the first night we met but I've been denying it, suppressing it or disguising it as something else. It was cruel of me to say I didn't love you back in Paris. I can never forgive myself for that. But I was so threatened by your desire to have another child. It made me shut down in a blind sort of panic.'

Could she believe him? Could she risk further heartbreak if she was wrong about his motives for being here?

'How do I know you mean it? You might be just saying it to get me to come back to you.'

His grip on her hands tightened as if he was worried she was going to pull away. 'I deserve your scepticism. The way I blocked any discussion about having another child was a knee-jerk reaction, sure, but it was unspeakably cruel to send you away as if I cared nothing. I love you with every beat of my heart. I can't imagine life without you by my side. It is no life without you. I'm a robot, a zombie like my father was when he lost my mother.'

'You're not just saying this because you want me back?'

'I'm saying it because it's true. I can't be who I'm meant to be without you. I never thought there was such a thing as a soulmate but I've realised you don't find a soulmate, you *become* one.' He squeezed her hands. 'I've become the man I want to be because of you. I didn't know I was capable of such depth of feeling.'

'Oh, Joe...' She blinked back tears. 'I'm so frightened I'm going to get hurt again. It was so hard losing both you and the baby.'

He brought one of her hands up to his mouth, his eyes holding hers in a tender lock. 'You're not going to lose me, *cara*. I will always be here for you, no matter what. I can't guarantee we won't lose another baby. No one can guarantee that, but what you can count on is this—I will be with you every step of whatever journey our lives take us on.'

Hope blossomed in her chest. 'So, are you saying you'd consider having another baby?'

He brought her closer, his eyes dark and tender, so full of love it made her heart turn over.

'I'll probably be a nervous wreck throughout your pregnancy, but it will be worth it if we are so lucky as to be blessed with a child. The thought of losing you like my father lost my mother haunts me. It haunted me from the start but when I visited my mother's grave the other day—'

'You visited her grave as well?'

Joe gave a rueful smile. 'It was long overdue but, yes, I did. It was strange. I didn't see it in the same way as I had as a teenager. I saw all those other graves—lives well lived, others cut tragically short—and I realised no one can guarantee you won't experience grief at some stage. Having another child will test me in ways I don't want to be tested. But it's part of being human to experience grief sooner or later. And being human, fully human, means being able to give and receive and openly express love.'

He stroked her face and looked deeply into her eyes.

'I love you so much. I can't bear the thought of spending however much time I have left on this planet without you by my side. I have already wasted too much of it without you. Come back to me, *tesoro mio*. Please?'

Juliette blinked back tears and flung her arms around his neck. 'I never want to be apart from you again. I love you. I've been so sad without you. So miserable and empty and lonely. But we can take our time having another baby. We don't have to rush into it.'

'We will try for another baby after we renew our wedding vows.'

Juliette blinked. 'You really want to do that?'

He grinned. 'Of course. We can even get Damon's cousin Celeste to organise it. It will be a celebration like no other. I'll give her carte blanche.'

Juliette gave a soft laugh. 'You don't have to do that. The simplest ceremony will do me. All I need to hear is you say the words and mean them.'

'I will love and honour and protect you until I take my last breath.' He brought his mouth down to hers in a lingering kiss that contained hope and love and healing. He drew back to gaze down at her once more. 'You have made me happier than I ever thought I could possibly be. I will always feel sad about our baby girl. Always—but that doesn't mean we can't build a wonderful life together. We will support each other during the bad times and celebrate the good ones.'

Juliette hugged him tightly, so full of love and joy it was hard to get her voice to work. 'I can't believe you actually love me. I still think I'm dreaming. That I will wake up and you won't be holding me like this—that I'll be alone again.'

Joe leaned down to kiss the tip of her nose.

'You're not dreaming, *cara mio*. I didn't know it was possible to love someone the way I love you. But if you need any more evidence...' He brought his mouth down to hers, his sexy smile sending a tickly sensation down her spine.

Juliette smiled and stood on tiptoe to meet his lips. 'I'm a big fan of evidence.'

EPILOGUE

April the fifth, the following year...

JOE CRADLED HIS newborn son in his arms and looked down at his beautiful but somewhat exhausted wife. After a mostly trouble-free pregnancy, Juliette had gone into labour the night before his birthday, and at ten minutes past midnight Alessandro Guiseppe Allegranza had been born.

'Isn't he gorgeous?' Juliette said, a dreamy expression on her face.

Joe rocked the little bundle in his arms, his heart feeling as if it was going to explode with love. 'He's amazing, like his mother.'

He stroked a careful finger over the minuscule face—the tiny button nose, the twin wisps of dark eyebrows, the soft downy black hair. It was a miracle to hold new life in his arms. A new life that repaired some of the pain of his own birth that had taken his mother from him. A new life that would help them move on from the loss of their first baby, Emilia. Not as a replacement—no child could ever be that—but as a new chance to experience all the joys and challenges of parenthood.

'Happy birthday, darling,' Juliette said, beaming.

Joe smiled so widely he thought his face would crack. 'I couldn't have asked for a better birthday present.' He looked down into his baby son's face. 'And you, little guy, couldn't have asked for a better mother.'

* * * * *

WE HOPE YOU ENJOYED
THIS BOOK FROM
(H)HARLEQUIN
PRESENTS

Escape to exotic locations where passion knows no bounds.

Welcome to the glamorous lives of royals and billionaires, where passion knows no bounds. Be swept into a world of luxury, wealth and exotic locations.

8 NEW BOOKS AVAILABLE EVERY MONTH!

#3805 THE SPANIARD'S SURPRISE LOVE-CHILD
Passion in Paradise
by Kim Lawrence

Softhearted Gwen had always dreamed of the day tycoon Rio would discover their child. Yet the reality is astounding! Because when the brooding Spaniard sweeps back into her life, he demands their daughter—and her!

#3806 MY SHOCKING MONTE CARLO CONFESSION
Passion in Paradise
by Heidi Rice

He's Monaco racing royalty and I, Belle Simpson, was his housekeeper. But that evening, Alexi's searing gaze exhilarated me. Five years later, I finally have the chance to reveal my secret—Alexi's a father!

#3807 A BRIDE FIT FOR A PRINCE?
Passion in Paradise
by Susan Stephens

Samia's thrilled by the longing Prince Luca awakens within her but knows a temporary fling is their only option. A future with him is impossible. For the shadows of her past make Samia wholly unsuitable...don't they?

#3808 A SCANDAL MADE IN LONDON
Passion in Paradise
by Lucy King

Kate is *mortified* when billionaire Theo discovers her secret dating profile. Yet she can't resist his tantalizing offer to introduce her to pleasure beyond her wildest imagination! But the biggest scandal of all is yet to happen...

YOU CAN FIND MORE INFORMATION ON UPCOMING HARLEQUIN TITLES, FREE EXCERPTS AND MORE AT HARLEQUIN.COM.

HPCNMRB0320

SPECIAL EXCERPT FROM

⊕HARLEQUIN

PRESENTS

*Theo has one goal: vengeance on his runaway bride,
Helena! But Theo can't escape the past...or the intense
connection that spectacularly reignites between them. Will
this tycoon be tempted to rewrite the rules of his revenge?*

Read on for a sneak preview of
Michelle Smart's next story for Harlequin Presents
His Greek Wedding Night Debt

Did she realize that every time she spoke to him, she tilted toward him? Did
she realize that she fidgeted her way through every conversation? Was she
aware that her breath hitched whenever he walked past her? Was she aware
that at that very moment her hands trembled?

"The next thing I wanted to discuss is the kitchen," she said, moving
the conversation on.

"What about it?" he asked lightly.

She tugged at the sheets of paper he'd placed his backside on. "You're
sitting on my notes."

"My apologies." Sliding smoothly off the desk, he went and sat on the
chair on the other side of her desk. "Is this better?" But she didn't respond.
Her eyes were on his, wide and stark, her fidgety body suddenly frozen.
"Helena?"

She blinked at the mention of her name and quickly looked down at
her freed notes.

"Yes. The kitchen." Despite Helena's best efforts, her voice sounded
all wrong.

It had been hard enough to breathe with Theo propped on her desk
beside her—when he'd first perched himself there, she'd feared her heart
would explode out of her chest—but when he'd moved off, she'd had to
fist her hands to stop them from grabbing hold of him. Now he was sitting
opposite her and she'd caught a sudden glimpse of his golden chest beneath
the collar of his polo shirt, and in the breath of a moment her insides had
turned to mush.

It shouldn't be like this, she thought despairingly. She'd spent three
months under Theo's intoxicating spell, riding the roller coaster of her life.

HPEXP0320

He'd had the ability to make her forget everything that mattered. Under his spell she'd believed all she needed was Theo in her life to be happy. She was sure her mother had once believed the same thing before she'd sold her soul to a monster. Theo wasn't a monster like Helena's father, but his power over Helena had been just as strong.

How could she still react so strongly to him? She'd believed the sudden detonation of their relationship had killed her feelings for him, but she saw now that she'd been hiding them, hiding them so deep inside that she'd forgotten how powerful they were until one look at him in the Staffords boardroom had seen them poke their heads out from dormancy. Now the old feelings were slapping her in the face, taunting her, and it was getting harder and harder to fight them.

Eyes now determinedly fixed on the papers on her desk, she rubbed the nape of her neck, cleared her throat and tried again. "We need to discuss the kitchen's layout. Do you still want to consult a professional chef about it?"

She knew the moment she said it that she'd made a mistake.

Something sparked in his eyes. He leaned forward a little, a satisfied smile spreading over his face. "You do remember."

"Only that neither of us can cook." She quickly fixed her gaze back on her notes, aware her face was flaming with color.

"But you asked—specifically—if I still wanted to consult a chef about the kitchen… What else do you remember?"

She tucked her hair behind her ear and wrote something nonsensical on her notepad. "Have you a chef in mind to consult?"

"Answer my question."

Her hand was shaking too much to write anything else.

"Helena."

"What?" Helena intended for her one-syllable question to come out as a challenge. She might have succeeded if her voice hadn't cracked.

"Look at me," he commanded.

Heart thrashing wildly, she breathed deeply before slowly raising her face. "What?"

His voice dropped to a murmur. "What do you remember?"

Trapped in his stare, she found herself unable to lie. "Everything."

Don't miss
His Greek Wedding Night Debt
available April 2020 wherever
Harlequin Presents books and ebooks are sold.

Harlequin.com

HPEXP0320

2653